# Soul-Singer

## of

## Tyrnos

# Soul-Singer

## of

## Tyrnos

---

A RDATH  M AYHAR

AN ARGO BOOK

Atheneum    1983    New York

*To my husband and sons,*
*who live among strange worlds*

Library of Congress Cataloging in Publication Data

Mayhar, Ardath.
Soul singer of Tyrnos.

"An Argo book."
Summary: Yeleeve, a young woman who can sing the image
of a soul onto the wall behind her, to commend or condemn
the owner, discovers that a powerful evil is overcoming her
country and only she can help.
[1. Fantasy] I. Title.
PZ7.M468So [Fic] 81–5023
ISBN 0–689–30852–3 AACR2

Published simultaneously in Canada by McClelland & Stewart, Ltd.
Composition by American-Stratford Graphic Services, Inc.,
Brattleboro, Vermont
Manufactured by Fairfield Graphics, Fairfield, Pennsylvania
Designed by Mary Cregan
First Printing July 1981
Second Printing January 1983

### HUYM
*Symbol of music and truth*

### LYIN
*Symbol of rulership*

# Contents

# Contents

*Soul-Singer*

*of*

*Tyrnos*

# 1

## *For the Last Time*

WHEN the chime rang for the last time, there was stillness. In the stone building that housed the Singers, the three notes rippled up the curving stairwells, fanned along the corridors. I felt my own breath stop for a heartbeat. From this day forward, my life and those of my fellows would be changed totally.

I moved through the door-curtain and found myself among many others who were robed in gray, as I was. The long folds billowed about us as we hurried silently down the stair to the Great Hall. *For the last time, for the last time,* I thought, as we poured through the doors in a gray tide and went to our knees on our kneeling-cushions.

As usual there was a long wait. I found myself studying the great map that followed the curve of the wall behind the tall chairs where the Teachers would sit. All the world of Riahith was drawn upon it, though in these latter days there are none who sail across the vast oceans to visit the continents that rim their other shores. Our own lands centered the map, and I found myself wondering what my own path through them would be, when we were given our assigned directions.

The ragged triangle of Malchion capped the continent, straggling upward into the Northern Seas, then widening downward to meet the mountains that divide it from our own Tyrnos. Our country bulged outward from the mountains to the sea, covering the western third of the landmass. Scarlet circles marked the four great cities that serve our sparsely populated country: Sarnos, to westward; Lilion, guarding the eastern border, high in the mountains between Tyrnos and Ageron, the land to the East; the Citadel, home of the High King, to south and east of our own location; Langlorn, on the southern sea.

Where would my own paths lie? That thought, I knew, lay in all our hearts. We knelt, a floorful of young men and women, quiet and disciplined. Yet our minds were already casting outward, wondering what labors lay before us to test the long schooling that we had been given.

There was a change in the pressure of the air around us. All stood in one effortless upward thrust of trained muscles. The three Eldest appeared behind their chairs as if by magic, so soundless had been their steps. Elysias, the Director, took her place in the center and touched the silver bell that hung in its half-moon frame. Its "ting!" sent us to our knees again, as Arnos sat himself to her left and Sirna to her right.

The voice of Elysias floated quietly upward, as we touched our fingers to our knees and bent our heads.

"Once again we have completed a Training," she sang. "Most High Gods, whose thought forms our world and all its fellows, look upon your new instruments and servants. They have come through years and trials and disciplines, leaving behind all that they were, all that they had. Even their names they now leave behind them, that they may not be tempted to glorify themselves."

Our voices joined hers, now, in affirmation, the harmonies finding themselves effortlessly, from long custom. Then the note died away.

Arnos touched the bell. "After so many years, you know your duties. Yet I shall define them once again, for the final

time. Yours is the task of keeping Tyrnos a place of justice, of
mercy, of good conscience. When you sing the soul of a noble,
it hangs there for all his folk to see in its uprightness or its
evil. If a soul revealed to be wicked remains unmended, the
High King is empowered to remove its owner from his place
of authority and to replace him with another.

"When you sing the soul of a landholder, the same holds
true. When you sing the souls of common folk, laborers or
serving women or bondsmen, it is given to you to set their
small warpings aright. You are not allowed to refuse the request of anyone. You are not allowed to pass any Great House
without presenting yourself for a Singing of its Lord or Lady.
And that Lord or Lady is not allowed to refuse your offer.

"Ours is the strangest calling in all the world of Riahith.
No other land is conducted by the laws that rule us. No other
folk produce those who, like you, are gifted with the Voice
that links you with the High Gods. You have given up much.
You are offered more." His voice stilled, and we hummed a
note of acceptance.

Sirna touched the bell. Her voice took up the tale. "The
gods have many servants," she said. "Common folk serve
them, though less knowingly than we. The living trees, the
very grasses of the meadow serve them. Beasts serve them.
Scorn no aid that is offered you, whatever the source. Remember that we who teach you do not know all that is to be known
of the gods and their kindred. A few of us, over the long years,
have encountered beings who are of the gods. She who was
once Soul-Singer to the High King set into the record that
above us is placed the One Who Watches All, who is neither
man nor woman, human nor beast.

"Take thought for those who seem strange or alien. Though
it has been known that Outsiders have touched our world,
those who are truly alien to us have not been met for many
lives of men. Those who serve the gods will touch a note of
gladness in your hearts."

Now Elysias rose to her feet, her blue robe with its silver Symbol flowing outward from her shoulders. Her voice deep with reverence, she said, "In every generation, one Singer is chosen by the gods for some terrible task. Often it is a task that we, who should be of the Wise, have not recognized as important. Seldom do the gods choose as we would choose, but their choice has never failed them.

"We who are Singers stand between our land and all its perils. Tyrnos needs no devices, for it has its Singers. Tyrnos has no army, for it has its Singers. Tyrnos needs no tight web of governors and enforcers, for it has its Singers. Every day we hold our land safe and strong and secure. Feel no shame if your calling is only that which comes to the common run. But if you are summoned to other tasks, feel no pride. It is simply your duty."

She touched the silver bell once again, and when its thin voice had died away the chairs were empty.

Then the map was lighted from within. My breath tightened in my throat. Now the time had come for each Singer to be given his direction. Tension filled the air as the first name was called, and a golden arrow shone on the map. Southwest, toward Sarnos and the Ocean. Another, and another, and another received their arrows. As each was directed, he rose and left the hall. Our ranks grew thinner. My name caught my ear, and I gazed at the map. North by east lay my path, then.

No cities lay in my way; not even any large towns were there. Only farmsteads and lordly holdings, forests and grasslands, almost-emptiness. Still I felt little disappointment. I was small; my voice was not yet powerful. I knew myself to be ignorant of many things. I had not expected to be sent to a great city.

I went straight to my sleeping mat. When I pushed aside the curtain to enter, I stopped in surprise, for Elysias herself stood in my narrow space. My mat was rolled away, and in its place was a small pack. Beside it were the leather tunic and trousers that all of my kind wore into the world, with a pair of heavy shoes beside them.

"I have come, Yeleeve, because I am compelled to," she said. "My thought has been with you since my finger first touched the bell. It is in my mind that you might be the Chosen of this generation, though why this should be I cannot imagine. Many of your class are finer Singers than you. Most are larger and stronger. Yet your name rings in my heart.

"If this be true, I must give you further instruction and advice. Know, Child, that while the gods can be tangible and humanlike, as you have been taught, they are much more than that fact would make it seem. They are not bound by flesh, as we are. They know more worlds than this, and our limited dimensions cannot hold them. They are outside time. They are not, in fact, physical beings, though they can seem so."

I opened my mouth to question, but she raised her hand.

"Wait. I am not done. Their ways are unlike our own. They may set you a task, but they will not make it easy or assure your success. And the penalty of failure will be death . . . or worse things. The tools and knowledge you will need will be available, but only your own courage and wit and determination will set them into your hands. Though it may seem that you are swept along by events, it will be only your own right choosing that leads you down the path that leads in the way of the gods."

I nodded slowly. "I must not *depend*, then on being shown the way. I must do what seems right—and hope that it will be . . ." I stood there, shaken by the sudden realization of what she had said.

"I was a Chosen," she said, taking my hand in both of hers. "It is a strange thing, but you will have no time to think of it. You will be tempted aside, it may be, or delayed or distracted; but the gods will not have it so. Take care what you do, Yeleeve. Follow your guides, whatever they may be. Trust in your own instinct. The gods do not choose unsuitable instruments."

She stooped and kissed my cheek. Then she was gone.

I settled my leathers about me, then took up the pack. I looked around the cell that had been mine since I was ten years old. Not one item lay in it that was mine. The stool, the mat, the pitcher were already anonymously waiting for their next user. I might never have spent a decade of my life sleeping in this spot. I straightened my shoulders under the pack, brushed aside the curtain, and moved into the hall.

The building was empty. I realized that my classmates had already gone their ways while I was detained by Elysias. This suited me, for I had found few among them who were better company than my own thoughts. We had been a solitary lot, as Singers must be, and our teachers had discouraged the forming of friendships.

I moved down the stair, and the sculptures of crystal glimmered in their niches as if to say farewell. The icy shapes had delighted me from the time when I had been forced to stand tiptoe to see them. I felt, rather sadly, that it was a strange thing that I regretted most the leaving of their cold forms.

In the passageway that stood between the arched portal and the Hall I found two who waited for me. Arnos and Sirna stood there, tall shapes in blue with the *Huym* symbol glowing on their robe fronts.

I stopped before them and bent my head for their blessings. Their hands moved, forming the *Huym's* lyre-shaped figure in the still air. Then Arnos stepped forward and spoke softly to me.

"We have felt a strange compulsion, Child. Always there are those whom we are saddened to see depart these walls. You have been such a one for your teachers. Elysias is puzzled at our intuition that you may be the Chosen, but we are not. Though you have been rebellious and strong-minded, we have valued your mind and your spirit. There is within you a toughness and determination that comforts our thoughts of you.

"We feel a premonition that you may face the most difficult task any Singer has faced in many generations. Go with the gods, Yeleeve. Go with our blessings." They moved their hands again, and the *Huym* gleamed faintly in the air that followed their motions.

I was strangely moved. There had been no affection offered or asked in all those long years. Respect had flowed between us in an unspoken current, but we had been set apart by years and training. I had not suspected that these two greatest of my teachers had held any special feeling for me.

I bent my head and murmured, "My thanks, Wise Ones. Hold me in heart." Then I turned and went down the corridor, out the tall portal, and into the Longroad that weaves together all the villages and holdings of our stingily-tenanted western hills.

I turned once. The School for Singers loomed behind me in the sun of noon, its smooth curves glistening as if gilded. The arched doors were shadowed by the carved portico, and the slender windows were shuttered with bars of shade. Its face seemed closed against me. I turned back to my way and did not look again.

That first day was a long one. No holding lay within a half-day's journey of the School, and only the curves of the hills, the windings of the road, and the occasional late-summer birds bore me company. Still I was not lonely. Loneliness is wrung out of the fibres of a Singer before childhood ends.

Night found me on the edges of grasslands that gave promise of being grazing grounds, though I could see no cattle. The over-warm day had given way to a breeze that promised to nip a bit before morning, so I took the plain cloak from my pack and spread it beneath a hedge that bordered the roadway. A handful of grass from the meadow made a pillow, and my resting place was ready.

After munching my dried fruit, I lay back to watch the stars through the thorny branches above me. For a moment I closed my eyes, and when they opened again it was dawn.

That morning I bitterly regretted my faithful washing pitcher. I felt as if the grime of years had crusted over my face, but I rose, folded away the cloak, and moved forward, watching for a sign of a dwelling or a stream. I suspected that my love of cleanliness might be sorely tried in my life on the road.

Before the sun was well over the line of low trees to the east, I saw a curl of smoke above a modest farmhouse. Then I hurried, and soon I was lifting the latch of the wooden gate that divided the garden walk from the road.

An army of geese set up a ferocious medley of honkings and hissings. The big white gander came forward, neck curled like a serpent, wings cocked for battle. I prudently stood where I was and called out, "Is anyone there? A Singer, new-come from the School, begs a bit of water for washing."

The door opened with a rush, and a pale woman fluttered into the yard. "Be'n a Singer, indeed?" she asked. "Th' gods ha' heard our cry. Come in, Singer, and be welcome. We've need of such as ye."

A moment of panic struck me. I had sung souls, true, but only under the eye of one or another of my teachers or Elysias. Never before had I been faced with total responsibility for the well-being of another person. Still, I kept my face calm as I followed the dame into her cramped home.

A long bony man lay on a low couch before the fire. His forehead was clammy to my touch, and his skin was prickled as if with chill, though the morning was already warm. His eyes were sunk beneath the brows, and their lids were bluish. He was very ill, I could see, though I had no training in physician craft.

"Good dame," I said, drawing her aside to the window,

"your man is ill, not troubled in his spirit. We who are Singers can do little for sickness of the body."

She looked at me with such uncomprehending faith in her eyes that I sighed and continued, "Yet I will try. But when I am done, find some person who can be trusted and send to the School for a healer."

She nodded and snapped her fingers. A small boy crawled down from an overhead loft and looked up at me. He seemed far brighter than his mother, so I told him, "Go to the School. If you run quickly, you will be there before dark. Tell them that a healer is needed and bring him back with you as soon as may be."

He nodded and set off with the air of one who knows what he is about.

Now I set my mind on the sick man. No living soul can take harm from being truly sung, and I comforted myself with that thought.

For the first time in my life, I felt the Power sing through me, unfiltered through the mind of another. I drew a deep breath, and the music took me in its grasp. There in that dark hut I sang, and the wan spirit of the man formed on the wall beside the hearth at my back.

It was a gentle singing. Cramped spaces eased; tensions were relaxed. Old worries were erased in that time while I sang. The wife stood in silent awe, staring at the shape behind me. I could see in her face the changes as they were made.

When I was done, the man lay deeply asleep, and it was a different sleep from that in which I had found him. I watched him for a time, making certain that all was as well as his sick body could manage. Then I asked the dame, "May I wash at your well? I have slept under a hedge, and water was not at hand."

She blushed crimson with shame. "I be out in my manners, Singer. Should be that I offered you food and drink before you made to sing. Now forgi' me. I'll warm water enough for a bath, while you eat'n your morning meal."

So I found myself sitting in the shade before the door with a tray of griddle cakes on my lap, watching the morning progress over the farmlands that now lay across my way. As I nibbled, listening to my hostess splash pails of water into the great iron tub over the fire, I suddenly realized that I was now, in very truth, a Singer of Souls.

# 2

## *Singer of Souls*

THE road curved away over the low hills, and the gray dust that marked its line blended with the autumn gray of dead grasses to make my way dreamlike and dim. Even the watery shining of the sun gave no color to the drab bushes and small trees that I passed from time to time. No longer was I a stranger to the road. My feet were shod in its dust, and no hint of the russet glow of my boots showed through its film. Yet the sight of their trim newness tore at my heart, for they had been given me by the household of Kalir.

Only the muted creaking of my leather jerkin and breeches marked my progress. I neither hummed nor sang, and more than one tear dropped to trace my path. Strange behavior for a Singer, I well knew. But seldom does a Singer remain long in one place and never as a part of one family, yet in the odd way I had followed since my leaving school, I had been long with Kalir and his people. Not, at first, by my own choice. Later, indeed, in disregard of my training and the warnings of my teachers and Elysias.

The summer had been full of joy. I remembered the warmth of the road dust on my sandaled feet on one special day, the summer bloom of the thornbushes that now were only twiggy ghosts of themselves. I had been singing them, working my perceptions deeper and deeper into the layered, unvoiced beings as I passed, exercising my gifts as a Singer should.

The thunder of hooves behind me did not interrupt my chant, though I moved to the verge of the road and turned to see who approached. A big man, a flash of orange beard, a wide-nostrilled chestnut, dripping with foam, loomed near. There was a laugh, and I was cast backward into the ditch and knew nothing for a black time.

Then Kalir and his merry-eyed dame and their boisterous brood found me and brought me to the few senses I had left, after striking my head upon a stone. They took me home with them, as they would have done for a beggar or a dog or even a noble who found himself in such unlikely straits. And my life among them began, full of new sensations, strange tasks, and emotional ties such as I had never known.

Without the week of rest that my injury demanded, perhaps I would not be have been seduced from my duty. For that length of time I allowed myself to sink into the family as if I had been born to them, and they accepted me as readily as I grew attached to them. If Elysias had said to me, "You are the Chosen. There is no doubt," I would have hardened myself and gone forward, when I was recovered. But she had not. She had said, "Might be." And that I was able to put from mind.

Few of my sort have ever known the joy of a family. We are taken away from our own, as soon as the talent shows itself, to the schools provided for us. There is a life there, of a kind. Sustenance for the body, long hours of work for the mind and the voice. Yet there is none of the closeness that a tight-knit family knows. So it was that the house of Kalir held wonder for me, as those loving folk enfolded me into their lives and their hearts.

For one used to the roads and the fields, the Singing-places of great houses and the chimney corners of humble dwellings, my time with Kalir was magical. I would look with wonder after Doni, the mother, as she chuckled about the house, supervising awkward young fingers in intricate stitches or unpracticed serving-maids in making new dishes.

Her patience made me marvel, as did her casual pats and sudden warm hugs as she passed me—or any of her loved-ones —about the house. And her husband was even more wonderful. I watched his broad figure move away to the fields in the morning with something like woe and saw it return at evening with the same squealing joy as did his own younglings. His laugh boomed among the smoke-dimmed rafters and made the smoked joints dance and the strings of onions sway in time with the loops of peppers.

The astringent life of the School seemed a dream. The thin, chill-voiced teachers, in retrospect, seemed to have no blood in their veins to work the metal pumps that were their hearts. I suspected that their passionless lectures upon the vital functions of Singers took root so deeply in our hearts only because no more exuberant seeds had been planted there.

So when Kalir and Doni and the seven children pleaded with me to forsake the road, my long training, and my sacred duty, I gave ear. My rebellious nature had always chafed at the duties laid upon me without my consent, and now I told myself that the lack of one Singer of so many thousands could make little difference in the safety and virtue of my country. The warning I had been given . . . "You may be tempted aside . . . but the gods will not have it so" . . . I tried to forget. The possibility of immediate joy, of belonging with these people who loved me was temptation beyond resisting.

Perhaps that was why the gods permitted that evil should befall even those whom they had earlier favored. On the first chill evening of autumn, while we sat before the great fireplace talking and laughing; while nuts sizzled and popped in the red coals, the doors burst inward, without warning. Armored men poured between the broken leaves, swords drawn. They spared neither Kalir nor his wife, children nor servants.

They ignored me, as they reddened their blades in the blood of those I loved. Though I had little skill in arms, I struggled with them and tried to skewer one with the meat spike from the fireplace. It almost seemed as if they could see me only dimly, for they flung me against the wall, half stunned, and then forgot me. I lay there and saw them at their bloody work, and the steel of the gods and the words of the Mother entered into me.

When their terrible task was done, they looted the house, taking hidden stores of coin from strange hiding places, as if they had known exactly where to look for them. Then they dragged the blazing logs from the hearth into the middle of the room. The ancient planking kindled, and evidence of the crime seemed likely to vanish in smoke. But I am a Singer, and I know the colors and emblems of every family above the fifth degree of nobility in all the land.

I recognized the work of Razul, even before I identified his shield upon the breasts of his henchmen. Any who wander farther than their own byre and wash place have heard whispers of his deviltries. Though I had never seen him, I knew him by his work, and I vowed to find him.

When I went forth from the burning house, my face was wet with tears and with blood. I had laid my cheek to the lips of every one of those who lay within, seeking the tiniest whisper of breath. There was not one who lived. I kissed Kalir upon the forehead and closed his eyes. I patted Doni, as she had so often patted me, and I touched each of the children on the brow and straightened their limbs, that they might go into the flame in good order.

Then, my hair singed and skin blistered, I made a vow,

signed in blood and flame, that Razul would pay to the utter-
most for this thing that he had caused to be done.

Singers are not trained with sword and bow. Far other are
our functions and our duties. Our hearts are cleansed of the
burning and the bitterness that make men kill, as much as can
be done with humankind. Though in the sharpness of my
wrath and the grief of my loss I would gladly have slain
Razul wtih my two hands, my long training overbore that
wild pain. By the time I had cleaned myself in the cattle
trough, I knew that I must fight Razul with my own weapons,
not with his.

So from that spot on the road where I had been taken up,
I set out again. This time I knew my destination. We are
taught to let the gods and the teachings of the Mother be
our guides, using our inner perceptions to determine our ways
and our means. I, more than most, had relied upon my own
judgments, to the distress of my teachers. Now I used all possible guidance, following into lanes and byroads and again
into a principal thoroughfare, knowing that I must be led to
Razul as a river is led to the sea.

The leagues rolled away beneath my boots, but I did not
grow weary. Children came into the road to ask me into farmsteads along the way. Sometimes I rested for the night or for a
meal, paying, as always, with a song that eased, perhaps, an
old grief or a new grievance. Even, once, I healed a cow that
was pining and going dry after the sale of her calf. Her soul
was such a simple pleasure to work into, after the murk of
human spirits: Food, water, sleep, sun, hands milking, the
spot where the calf had been.

But my russet boots moved on, and the miles curled up behind me like lengths of used-up ribbon. At last I came to
Raz, the village that lay about the Great House of Razul. The
house stood amid its stern turrets, protected by strong walls,
but Raz was a scabrous place, filled with two- and four-
legged rats. The men who stood about the filthy wineshops

scratched themselves and leered when I passed, though a Singer is protected by every law that men and the gods can devise.

Though my dress and bearing might well have been those of a young man, still I was followed by a verminous taggle of urchins and ill-looking men. I was glad to reach the wall gate, where an armed watchman was on guard. He seemed puzzled by me and my request for entry.

"Surely you know the Singers of Souls," I said to him, astonished. "We are charged with the well-being of Tyrnos, and I am required by law to stop and to inquire if your Lord has need of my services. Not lightly does a Lord decline the services of a Singer." I drew my brows together, and the man touched his helm and went to inquire.

I waited, but I felt the beginning of the Power pulse in my veins. I knew that I would be admitted. When the guard returned, he gestured for me to come in, and a woman was waiting inside the gate to show me the way. She led me to the women's quarters of the house and showed me the bathing pool.

"You may borrow fine robes for your Singing, should you wish it," she said.

I smiled at her. "None sees the Singer while he sings, my friend, else he has failed in his art. If you will but rub the dust from my leather garments, I will be grateful to you."

The water in the pool was warm, but as I lay in it I felt a sudden chilly impotence. What could I, alone and unarmed, do against this powerful Lord, surrounded by his warriors and his women? The water swirled around me, comfortingly. I heard the voice of a teacher of long ago saying, "We are armed, Singers, with such weapons as soldiers do not recognize. We may come openly into any hall, any home, any chamber, and none will fear us. Yet we have in our hearts the Power. With it we may work the will of the gods."

When I climbed from the pool, the woman was waiting

with my jerkin and breeches, and she had rubbed them with sweet oil.

"We have never had a Singer of Souls here in all the time since I came," she said wistfully. "Is there nothing I can do for you?"

"Surely, if you wish it. I am hungry with my journeying. To sing well, I must have good food to sustain me. Can you find meat and bread, perhaps? Or cheese, or chicken?"

She smiled. "Food will be here in a short time, for I guessed that you hungered. Then it will be the hour for lighting the torches. Your time to appear before the Lord Razul . . ." She hesitated, looking closely into my eyes as if to gauge my soul. "Is it as I have heard? Can the Singers, in truth, change the hearts of evil men?"

I took her hand. "The Singers call upon a Power beyond themselves. That Power judges the one whose soul is sung. It sets his reckoning. The Singer cannot know beforehand what will take place when he sings. Still, evil souls have been changed, good souls made better, the treacherous exposed, and the cruel punished in the Singing places of their own houses."

She looked a bit frightened. But with it she looked gladdened. "The House of Razul," she whispered, barely perceptibly, "has suffered for want of a Singer."

With torchlight came a messenger from the Lord. I went forth to my lonely battle. Little did the Singing place resemble a battlefield: it was a round platform of polished stone set against the curved end wall of the feasting chamber of the House. An ornate stair curled about the column that held it up, and when I had mounted to the top, I found myself two man-heights above the floor.

The chamber was full of people. Men-at-arms mingled with nobles, ladies, and women (I guessed) of easy virtue. A few servants scurried among them, bringing wine cups and carrying away the remnants of the meal they had just finished. Upon an elevated dais sat Razul in a thronelike chair. The torchlight was brilliant, and I looked closely at him, while the crowd settled into something like silence.

I knew him! That curling orange beard (somewhat stained, now, with wine), the mouth that must snick like steel when he closed it. Those no-colored steely gray eyes had mocked me from the back of the horse that ran me down, and now they stared at me from deep in their sockets, like twin animals in their lairs. His attitude seemed relaxed, but I sensed a wariness about him as he looked across the wide chamber.

Deep within my heart, I said to the gods, "This is no vengeance of my own, for until this moment I did not know that the man I sought was the same who injured me." I took a deep breath, feeling the Power building within me, tingling along my nerves, the veinings of my body, the chambers of my heart. I held the breath for a long moment. Then I sang.

As always, the world disappeared, the hall, the feasters with it. Only the truth of the being who called himself Razul existed in all the Cosmos. And I sang his soul.

As my voice rose and fell, crescendo, tremolo, diminuendo, the shape of Razul's self formed upon the polished wall above and behind me. Though my back was toward it, I knew every line and tint of it, for the Power was shaping it, and I was the instrument of the Power.

Dimly, I was aware of a concerted gasp from the crowd, but I sang on. The bestial shape grew in foulness; the colors dripped with scarlet and purple. I heard a scream. The air about me was charged with fear and revulsion, but still I sang. The eyes of Razul hid in their twin lairs, but sparks of pain and rage escaped from that darkness. Had I not been trained, I might well have wilted in that glare, but I did not.

I sang the song to the end. Upon the wall in indelible hues was the thing that was the Lord Razul. Even his henchmen shrank from that image. Even the harlots at his side looked upon it with loathing.

When my voice fell silent, there was no sound in all the place except the sobbing breaths of Razul. He sat and looked upon the thing he had allowed himself to become, and it glowered from the wall, soul's twin to him.

For long heartbeats the world stood frozen as if time had ceased to tick away. Then Razul rose from his chair. He raised his clenched hands as though to challenge the beast on the wall. An inarticulate roar of pain ripped his throat. An emerald flashed in his dagger hilt, as he drew it from his sash. The glow was quenched in his blood.

He stood, bleeding his life away, staring at the thing on the wall. No soul stirred to aid him or to comfort him until he fell, as does a tree, full-length on his face.

Then there was hubbub, indeed. Women shrieked. Men cried out. Guards rushed in from the outer keep, weapons ready for battle, and joined the moil below.

I waited quietly, and sorrow filled my heart. How direful to be unable to live with the thing you have made yourself become! Kalir and his folk had died in the fullness of love and kindness, sent to the gods before their times, perhaps, but whole and at peace with themselves. This unhappy soul went forth into what dark limbo of self-rejection? Sad. Sad.

When the confusion was at its height, I went down the steps to the chamber. None stayed me or, indeed, seemed to see me. I remembered something the teachers had said . . . something about the gods holding their hands over those who work their will.

Anna waited in the passage with a heavy cloak and a pack of food. "Go with our blessing, holy one," she whispered.

I touched her forehead with my lips, took the parcel, and set my feet again upon the twilit road.

# 3

## *Daymare*

I WALKED away from chaos, into the lonely quiet of the road. Behind me rose the hubbub of men left suddenly leaderless, and I knew with certainty that future granny tales would tell of some fearsome warrior who came, armed and mighty, to unseat the terrible Razul.

I laughed. None would ever believe that it was only I, small and young and a woman, too, who had been the instrument of that Lord's doom. Still, that was my task, the fate of those who must be Singers.

Though I had come to the city of Raz in the grip of grim purpose, now I went away from it in the twilight with no destination in my mind. All ways are alike to a Singer, and we must trust to the gods to lead us toward the work they hold ready for our hands.

The dust puffed away from each russet boot as I walked. I looked up toward the darkening horizon and saw that it might well turn into mud, for purple-gray cloud hung there. It raced the night down-country toward me.

To my right, a few rods from the verge of the road, was the hem of a considerable wood that seemed to stretch in ever-thicker reaches until it filled the whole prospect to the south. Deciding that its shelter would be preferable to the exposed road, I turned aside and made my way among the slim young saplings of its outer edge until I reached the greater boles that marked the beginning of the real forest.

The strange stillness that precedes a storm held the wood in a fragile trance. My steps did nothing to break the waiting mood, as I made my way into the dimness of the ways beneath the heavy-leaved spread of branches that roofed out the sky. Finding, by touch, a hollow in a giant trunk, I rattled a dead branch inside to frighten away any resting serpent. Then I climbed into the gap, glad to find so secure a haven from the rain and the night that was now upon me.

I did not touch the wheel of my lightglass. There was some mood of darkness and quiet in that place that I felt would not take kindly to the intrusion of my kind. Instead I settled my bones among the twiggy debris that lay on the floor of my nook and closed my eyes, glad enough for the chance of rest, though I still felt the Power tingling along my nerves in faint echoes.

A crash of thunder and the chill mist of rain blown into my hiding place woke me. As I peered out, I could see the area about my tree kindled to wet-silver brightness by a flash of lightning. And more than trees and vines and fallen trunks were thereby revealed.

. I looked closely, not to miss the next lightning bolt. All through the wood, as far as I could see, there were dark forms, shapeless as though hooded and cloaked in black, moving through the sheeting rain, standing as though looking upward toward the shouting sky, or drifting into an eddy that seemed to center upon the tree in which I lay.

I closed my eyes and drew upon the residue of Power that still thrummed within me. I traced glowing bars of force across the opening behind which I lay, crosshatched them with others, and set at the webbed center the *Huym*. Without further worry, I slept again, lulled by the drumming of the rain and the swishing of branches.

When I woke, a shaft of pale sunlight was striking into my refuge. I stretched and climbed down onto the soaked mold of the forest floor, examining it closely for any trace of those dark watchers of the night before. The rain had been heavy and long, and if there had been any mark of foot or paw it was obliterated now.

Drawing from my pack a chunk of cheese and a heel of good bread, I stood and ate, surveying my surroundings carefully. Though there seemed nothing amiss, still there was a feel to that wood that made my neck hairs rise. Though I made no stir or movement more than was necessary, I could hear no bird, see no motion anywhere about me. Such an old forest should have been astir with small creatures: rabbits scuttling through the undergrowth, beetles champing noisily at the fallen and lichenous logs, birds feeding in the upper reaches. There was nothing.

A clatter of hooves over a stony patch in the nearby road distracted me, and I moved to the edge of the trees to see who was coming so swiftly. Away toward the towers of Raz, now out of sight behind the fold of low hills, the road was awash with morning sun. Drawing near upon it was a pony bearing a youth who flogged it without mercy, urging it to more speed.

Suspecting that I was the object of his pursuit, I stepped into view and raised my arms high, that he might see me. He reined in the pony and walked it through the young growth to the spot where I stood. As he drew near, I saw that he was, indeed, very young . . . more than twelve, perhaps, but less than fourteen. His milk-pale skin was blotched with cinnamon-colored freckles, and his hair was red-gold in the light.

As he approached, I saw his eyes widen and a look something like awe overspread his features. He sprang from the pony's back and knelt at my feet, making obeisance as though I were one of the High Adept, rather than a very young Singer clad in leather.

"You slept the night in the accursed wood?" he asked, as I lifted him to his feet and looked into his face. "None but the very wise and the terribly wicked can sleep safely there. My mother—" He choked as if to quell a sob, then continued, "My mother is like to die, because her mare carried her into that forest and dashed her head against a limb, knocking her senseless."

"Surely no wood can be blamed for a frightened horse," I murmured. "Such accidents happen everywhere, to all kinds of folk who never saw this wood."

"Not of the injury is she like to die," he said. "When they told me in the town that a Singer had come and gone, I came after you as fast as Cherry could gallop. I knew that you, if anyone alive, may be able to save her. May I sit and tell you of our trouble?"

So we sat at the edge of the road, as he feared to go into the trees, and he told me this tale:

"My father is from home, having been called by the High King to come down to the Citadel in the south. My mother, with his leave, wished to visit Grandam, who lives in Raz. Even Razul would not dare meddle with those of our family, and both knew that she could safely make the journey. We came past this wood on our way; we made our visit and persuaded Grandam to return home with us. Again we made to pass this wood, but a great black shadow rose beneath the hooves of Mother's mare, and she fled into the wood, mad with fear.

"We took Mother up, Grandam and I and the servants, and bore her home. It is not far, and there we brought her to herself. She seemed a bit dazed, but not seriously hurt. We were well content, for a time. But she had not known, before my father left, that there would be a new babe. He has not returned, though there has been more than enough time for him to end his business with the High King. She has grown wild and pale and weak. She calls for him in the night and speaks strangely of people in the wood.

"Our folk, though not wicked, are very fearful of things they cannot understand. They are talking among themselves, saying that the child to come is not of my father's get, but a demon begotten on my mother in the accursed wood. They will not listen to a youngling like me. They hardly listen to Grandam, though she is tall and fierce and can quell them, for now. They want to slay the child, though it means slaying Mother as well. She will not stay them, for she fears, too, that the child is not of human kind. Twice she has eluded her nurses and gone into the village to those who would take her life. Both times, thanks be to the gods, we overtook her and brought her safely back. Still, we know that we must have help, and I went to Raz to find a physician. When I learned that you had been there, I knew that the gods held us in their hands."

Here the boy paused, and I looked at him long. "I am surprised that any remembered that I was there," I said. "Few seemed to see me, even as I sang. Afterward . . . afterward no one but Anna, the serving woman, could see me at all."

"But it was Anna I went to," he said. "She is Nurse's sister, and she told me which way to go. Will you come with me to my father's house and see to my mother? The folk will surely listen to a Singer of Souls."

"I will come," I said. "But first I must cleanse this wood. If it reaches out and draws victims to it, it must not be left to do further wickedness. Tell me how to come after you, then go and spread the news of my coming. I will be there shortly."

The boy stood up from the stone upon which he sat. His hair flamed in the sunlight, and he said firmly, "Rolduth, Rellas's son, does not leave a maid alone to do a fearsome work. What help I can give you, I will."

I did not smile, for he was much in earnest. "Then come with me into the wood, Rolduth. Take my hand . . . no harm will come to you, that I swear."

26

## 3 · *Daymare*

He turned even paler than was his natural hue, but he took my hand. Together, we went into that still forest. When we reached the small clearing before the hollow tree, I stopped in the middle of it and turned to my companion. With my forefinger, I drew the Seal upon his forehead.

"Close your eyes, Rolduth. Stand firm, no matter what you hear or feel or touch. No matter what pictures form behind your eyelids. Your strength, added to my own, will make this task easier, leaving me more for healing your mother."

He looked about the clearing, which seemed very innocent, now, in the morning light. He nodded and closed his eyes. His warm, grubby hand held mine tightly.

I took a deep breath and held it. The Power surged, and I sang. As if a ground mist sprang into being, a haze filmed over the wood. In the mist walked the shapes of men and women. Some held up their hands, pleading; many cringed as if from blows; all seemed hunched and twisted with fear or pain. The sounds of whips cracking popped dimly in my ears. Ragged cries and tortured screams wove pale echoes through the wood. Murders were done before my eyes . . . and things more atrocious. I knew that I stood in a place unhallowed by ancient cruelties, and I sang more strongly still.

The Power leaped in me until I saw its dim haze stand out from my body as an aura. I sang sleep. I sang peace. I sang the death that ends all cruelties. By little and by little, the shapes became fewer, the sounds thinned to nothing, the haze drifted away on a little breeze that came wandering through the leaves. We stood, after a time, in a peaceful hollow where blue flowers peeped from hanging vines, even in this autumn season. Above us, where the sun shafted through, a shadow flickered, and I looked up in alarm. It was only a bird . . . the first one, I had no doubt, in years beyond counting.

The boy opened his eyes and again looked about the place where we stood.

"Is it done?" he asked, and I nodded.

"Now we will go to your mother," I said, loosing his hand from mine. "Your strength was of much help to me, Rolduth, son of Rellas. I am proud to have had you beside me."

He flushed with pleasure, and we walked to the road, leading the still-winded Cherry. The morning was not far advanced, though to me it seemed to have been long, indeed. Still, we made good time, though I was a bit fatigued after cleansing the wood. His young legs outpaced mine, his impatience speeding my own efforts.

Truly it was not far to the house of Rellas. Well before noon we topped a slow rise of land, and Rolduth touched my arm, pointing down into the wide valley that lay below us.

"There is my home. The Watchers will see us and tell my Grandam that we are coming. Do you mind, Singer, if I ride ahead and tell her first?"

I waved him on and kept my even pace, for too much haste disorders the mind and heats the blood. So I was taught, and so I have found it to be, when one must put forth much energy in one's work. As a result I found myself met, at some distance from the village wall, by a lady of fine aspect and searching eyes.

She was tall, and though her hair was streaked with gray it was still dark, matching her eyes. She strode out with a long, free gait, more like a boy than a grandmother. When we met, she clasped my hands in her own and smiled down at me.

"Well come, Singer. The gods, pardoning our doubts and our fears, send us aid at the hour of our greatest need. Enter our village and be at peace."

I returned her clasp and moved with her through the silent and staring folk, up the well-gravelled street, to the house of Rellas. It was no castle, nor even a Great House like that of Razul. Yet it was large and airy, made with some eye to grace and nice proportion. There were a few servants, but they were not cowed or fearful, and they met me with warm water for washing.

We ate the noon meal in cheerful talk of the road and the weather. So well-mannered was my hostess that she made no more mention of her worry until all my needs were met. Ther she led me into a small chamber, hung with embroideries and furnished with cushioned chairs and low worktables strewn with handwork and carefully copied books.

"Rolduth has told you of our trouble," she began, as we sat. "Some skill I have in soothing disordered spirits, for Raz is a disorderly place, with much head-cracking among the low, and more subtle wounds in those higher on the social scale. But my daughter has a wound I cannot heal. The blow to the head may be the sole cause, yet I believe it to be more. The accursed wood plays some part in her delirium. Unless she can be helped, she will escape our care and throw her life away."

I nodded. Looking her in the eyes, I said, "I have never tended such a case, being young in my profession. You may know that our training lies mainly in the direction of calling up the consciences of the powerful into the scrutiny of their subjects. But a spirit is a spirit, be it born or unborn, living or dead. The wood was filled with uneasy spirits and soaked in old horrors, yet I was able to sing it to rest. With the gods aiding me, I may be able to do the same for your daughter. But will that be enough, Lady? Will the villagers accept her assurances? Think on it, while I go to see her."

I went through the door she indicated, leaving the Lady Meltha with a thoughtful look on her face. The inner chamber was cool and dim, for thick draperies were drawn across the windows, though I could see by their motions that the shutters were open to the mild fall day. In a large bed against the unwindowed wall lay a young woman . . . almost too young, it seemed to me, to be the mother of so big a boy as Rolduth.

Her eyes turned toward me as I entered. Even in the darkness, I could see that she possessed a glory of red-gold hair and large eyes that seemed bottomless, as gray eyes often do. Without speaking, I went to the window and opened the curtains, letting the glow of noon sun pour into the room.

She turned away with a protesting gesture. I went to her and took her hand. "Lady Felisa, I am a Singer of Souls. I have come to help you determine if the child you carry is or is not what you fear it may be."

Her breathing eased, and the wild look left her. She stared at me searchingly, and I could feel her relaxing, bit by bit.

"Can it be done now?" she asked, and there was desperation in her voice.

"It can. But you know that there is unrest among the people in the village. Would it not be better to go out into the Mother Chapel there, and in the presence of all who can enter to sing the soul of your unborn child?"

"If I were certain of the outcome, I would say yes. If I should, indeed, be carrying a demon-child, I fear for your life and those of my mother and son. The folk are ignorant, though we try to teach them. They cling more to the earth-demons than to the teachings of the Mother and the beings of the gods. When they are filled with fear, they are most dangerous." Her voice carried away as a weary whisper, but I nodded again.

"Then we must first make a determination here. Do you want your mother and your son?"

"My mother. I fear to have my son . . . see . . . ."

So, with the Lady Meltha at my side, I stood for the second time in the same day and called upon the Power. My weariness seemed to be no obstacle, for the pulsing tensions built within me to override any failing of the flesh. My long breath, held for a heartbeat, came forth in a note so soft that it was barely within range of hearing. A crooning melody took me, and I sang.

I had never sung the soul of a child. I expected it to be small, but it was not. It was, perhaps, more *tender,* but there was no difference in the size of the impulse I felt.

On a spot on the wall, a shape appeared. A sad shape, it seemed, tentative and uncertain. Its short history shone within it, from the first pulse of life when it was only a mote of matter within its mother. Shadows appeared and disappeared. I guessed that these were stresses that had troubled Felisa and were conveyed to her infant through her own system. Then a tremendous shadow rose up and engulfed that glow of life, almost extinguishing it. As if a dark hand had twisted it, its shape changed, and a blot of darkness seemed to grow within it.

I reached out my hand and took Meltha's. She gripped firmly, and her warm strength was added to the Power and my own faltering energies. Again I breathed deeply. Then I sang a note of exultation, of triumph over darkness, of affirmation of life. A song of joy gripped me. As I sang, I saw the dark blot fade, slowly, and the twisted shape grow round and complete again. The glow brightened to glory, and as the song ended it winked out.

I fell at the Lady Meltha's feet, wrung dry by the exertions of the day. She lifted me to the bed beside her daughter and put a cool cloth to my cheek.

"Well done, Singer," she said. "So it was a human child, Felisa. You felt its warping by the dark forces of the wood and feared it a demon . . . and who is to say that the fears of the folk might not have been justified, had it come to birth unhealed?"

Felisa bent over me, her eyes filled with worry. "Have you come to harm, Singer?" she asked.

"No harm," I breathed. "But I fear I will have no strength for another singing for a time. Will the people wait?"

The sound of booted feet moved in the antechamber, and the door was quietly opened. Felisa gasped beside me; then she was up and moving into the arms of a stocky man who gladly received her there.

With admirably few words, Meltha told him what was needful. I asked again, as he digested that strange mixture of tragedy and hope, "Will the people wait?"

He looked down at me and made a strange little salute, as from one warrior to another.

"The people will wait," he said.

# 4

## *The Winter Beast*

I WAS a long time in the house of Rellas. Even after the folk had seen the soul of the unborn child sung upon the polished wall of their own Mother Chapel and had accepted its humanity, the Lady Felisa clung to me. Her mother, her husband, and her son added their pleas to hers, so I stayed well past my time, though I remembered too well the penalty of making my stay permanent.

Still I was not truly idle. Much was to be learned from Rellas, in those lengthening fall evenings, about his journey to the Citadel and the strange manner in which he had been detained there. His summoning had been unnecessary, by any reckoning. His taxes had been properly totaled and paid, and the services of a courier could easily have taken the necessary proofs to the capital city. So flimsy was the pretext upon which he had been taken from his home, so oddly disturbing was the collection of excuses that had been used to keep him in the Citadel, that I felt a frightening unease.

At the risk of seeming to overstep my place, I found an opportunity to talk with him about my forebodings. It was the night before my departure, for I knew the time had come for me to set foot again in the road. Felisa, now heavy with child, had gone to her chambers, with her mother to talk with her until she slept. Rolduth was in the stables currying Cherry. Rellas and I sat alone before his broad hearth, both of us feeling a bit saddened that my task with his family was done.

As a log broke into glowing halves, sending up a thousand red sparks to cling in the soot of the chimney wall, I asked him, "My friend Rellas, were you released to return home, or did you come unbidden, knowing that you must be needed?"

He looked at me strangely. "They would have kept me there until spring," he said. "As it was, I felt much unease, and I resented my time's wasting, there on the doorstep of the High King. He, having brought many forth from their places, would consent to see none of us. At last I visited Ernethos, the Scholar, who counseled my father before me. Though he is now withered and white-haired, his old head holds more knowledge of the usages of laws and the whims of men than any I know.

"He said to me, 'Rellas, if you abstain from visiting any of the Ministers, if you send no messages to the High King, for two weeks, they will check to ascertain your presence. After that you may go where you will, for they will assume that you are waiting quietly upon their pleasure. It may be months before you are missed.'

" 'But what if I am missed . . . what if they seek to trouble me concerning my going home without leave?' I asked him.

" 'You break no law now or ever upon the scrolls of the Citadel,' he said. 'Some mischievous quill-scribbler has taken it in mind to harry honest men. You are in no peril from the law.'

"So I did as he said, and after two weeks I set out for home . . . not an instant too soon." He sighed. "But I would have taken oath that our land was not conducted so."

Hesitantly, I shook my head. "There are ill things afoot, I am afraid. Others along my road had been summoned to the Citadel. None being as highly placed as you, they were astonished at the summons. Being mostly those who live by their own toil, they sent word that they could not come, for their families would hunger in their absence. But I wonder, Rellas, how many of them would have found it difficult to come home again?"

We sat for a long moment before I again took courage and spoke. "I think you should take care. Watch those who go and come upon the road through your lands. Any who stop, noble or common, should be judged warily and trusted not at all.

"I stayed for a time in a house of some wealth, though not a noble one. My stay ended when the men of Razul broke in our door and slew them all before my eyes. They knew where the small store of gold was hidden, though none who knew Kalir and his family, servant or friend, would have betrayed that good man.

"I sang the soul of Razul, and he troubles the ways no more; but I wonder . . . I wonder. Tyrnos, even with its Singers to keep men and women virtuous, has ways of dealing with such people as that villain. There was no need to wait until a Singer happened along. Why did the King, even at a distance in the Citadel, not know what all knew for leagues in any direction? And, knowing, why did he not send troops to bring Razul before him to answer for his crimes? The King's Guard is large enough to spare some few for such a task."

We looked eye into eye for a long moment, while the fire snapped and began to die away. Even with that warmth before us, with the cheer of the lamps blazing on their brackets, I felt suddenly chilled.

Rellas shivered as he sat. "When a land grows corrupt, too often the rot begins in high places. Not only the lowly may practice treason." He fell silent, fingering the braid on his sleeve and looking into the red coals.

"It may be that I have made a specter of a mere shadow," I said. "Still, caution is never harmful, if practiced wisely. Take care, my friend. You have more to lose than most . . . and your folk in the village are used to fair dealing and honest words. How would they prosper with . . . another sort?"

His square face flushed, where before it had been dyed red by the firelight. "It would go ill with them," he whispered. "They are only now losing the ignorance that has clung about them for generations. They are apt to trust the untrustworthy and to be suspicious of the true. An unloving lord would set them back into the old wretched mold."

"Then take care," I said. He was nodding as we both rose, and I went to rest with an easier mind than I had known in days.

It was a sad parting. Still, plead as they would, I knew that I could never forsake the road again. Perhaps the fate of Kálir's folk had been a quirk of the fates. Perhaps not. I was not going to chance a repetition of that, through my own fault.

In the few weeks I had spent housed and cossetted, the year had turned. Though the mang trees still held their heavy mats of leafage, to sigh and whisper until the buds of spring pushed them from the branches, the leaves had lost the autumn gold and were now gray-tan and sodden wtih cold rain. The road was wet beneath my russet boots, and I was glad that the gravelly soil of this region made it less a sea of mud than others I had walked.

The wind was fitful. When its gusts caught me, the chill cut through even the fur cloak that Felisa had made for me in place of the woollen one I owned. Though I had rested from the road, I had not sat idle; with Rolduth and Meltha I had exercised every day. Thus the doldrums had not crept into my muscles. I stepped along at my usual good pace, and that helped to warm me, once my blood began to sing along my veins. Still, the day was cold, and the approaching evening looked to be colder still.

I was moving, now, through wooded lands, uncut since the

beginning. The huge boles of the mangs colonnaded the way, and their reaching arms overarched the road. So thick was the wood that no undergrowth cluttered the forest on either hand. Darkness began to gather in those quiet aisles, and even the fitful jeering of grimbirds that had accompanied my progress died away into stillness.

It was old, old, and deep with ancient secrets—and perhaps some secrets not so ancient, for I felt a strange pulse beneath the level of conscious perceptions. Still, its heart was sound, though cloaked in mystery. I felt little wariness as I began to search its deeps with my eyes, seeking a spot in which to sleep warmly, sheltered from the cold night.

I had no taste for spending the blustery hours of darkness in a treetop. Though I knew that most of the forest's beasts had gone into their winter sleep, it would not be wise to tempt any late waking carnivore. The drifts of last spring's discarded leaves were damp and musty, uninviting in the extreme. I wanted a hollow tree, much like that which I had used before.

For so old a forest, it was remarkably healthy. No trace of rot appeared on any trunk within eyeshot. Sighing, I forsook the road and made my way beneath the rooflike limbs, looking sharply at every tree. I walked for some time, winding about but keeping my sense of direction firmly in hand. As the last light faded, I found a hollow, higher than was convenient but deep and floored with the dust of rotted wood and fallen bark.

Weary after my day's walk and my strenuous climb to my sleeping place, I spread my cloak, ate a bit from the generous store Meltha had supplied, and rolled that furry garment about me, head to heel. The wind rose with the coming of night, and I lay in that hospitable nook listening to its muttering among the leaves. When rain began to patter, I fell snugly into sleep.

No dream disturbed my rest. I woke to a magical morning: the rain had frozen in falling, and the forest was sheathed in ice. Its lanes were enchanted avenues from some mythical tale for children. I considered staying where I was, warm and sheltered, with enough food for many days. The footing, I knew, would be insecure and the ways treacherous with ice.

Something compelled me on my way, however, and it was not solely the plan that I had begun to formulate after hearing the tale of Rellas's journey to the Citadel. I had determined to direct my steps in that direction, for no one sets the path of a Singer. Not one of my teachers or even the administrators of my order knew where upon the lands I now stood. My way was my own, subject only to the calls of duty and to the instinct that Singers are taught to recognize.

I would go southward. Though I had had my training at a lesser School for Singers in the west of Tyrnos, I knew that I might claim a place for rest in that great mother of Schools in the country's capital city. There I might obtain answers to the many questions that had risen into my heart since the beginning of my wanderings. If not, I might observe simply if any canker might be eating its way into the very institution that had made Tyrnos the most lawful and kindly of nations.

I must not linger, be the weather what it would.

It was no easy matter to descend the ice-coated tree trunk. As it was, I slithered a few feet, then dropped unceremoniously onto my backside, gaining no few bruises in the fall. Setting my pack and my cloak to rights, I looked about to find the landmarks that would set me back on the way to the road.

Though the icy sheathing made everything appear different, there was no disguising the lightning-stricken snag that was my first marker. Confidently I moved toward it, caught my bearings, and veered away to the left, sighting on a mossy boulder. From landmark to landmark I went, never doubting that the memorized route would return me to the road I had left the night before. My confidence was ill-placed. When I reached the double-trunked mang tree that had been my first checking place after leaving the way, I looked expectantly past it.

There was no break in the wood. The wheel-and-hoof-worn track that I had followed had disappeared from my sight. Unmarked forest rose all about me, and I knew that if this was some mischief set upon my vision, I could never discover, so blinded, the winding way that I had never traveled before.

Roads do not evanesce in a night. Years may blur and obliterate their traces, but one night's rest cannot encompass such a thing. I frowned. Some thought had been laid over my path . . . some compelling spell had either deceived me into believing that there had been a road or was now deceiving me into believing that there was not. There was no evidence that I could lay tongue to, but the well-honed instincts that my teachers had spent ten years of my life in sharpening cried out to me, "This is witchery . . . or worse!"

I looked about. Icy-bright trees bent their heavy branches low on all hands, and the sharp cracks of overburdened limbs breaking sounded all around me. A snapping warned me, and I looked upward.

The double-trunked tree under which I stood gave a ripping groan, and one of the great halves swayed. I leaped for my life, turning in time to see the crystal-enclosed giant crash down upon the spot where I had stood.

Now my breath came hard, with shock and anger. More than a thought had been laid against me. A curse was moving in the wood, and I had no doubt that I was its specific target. I must win clear of the threatening branches or risk an end to my quest and my life. Not for this had I taken the hard lessons of the Singers' School to heart. I would bow my neck to no ill spirit that cast its spell across Tyrnos.

I stood still in the cleared spot left by the falling tree. Closing my eyes, I called upon the Power that I had never before been forced to use in my own behalf. A half-chant rose in my throat, and the strange sensations that were the tracks of the Power flowed through me. As if doubly frozen, the forest quieted until the faint chiming of ice against ice as the slight breeze moved through laden twigs was all that could be heard.

Into that quiet came the sound of steps. Not the two-footed steps of humankind, but a complex four-pawed gait that would have been padding, but for the crisp layer of ice upon the fallen leaves.

The sound neared, and I wondered behind my closed eyelids what beast still wandered the wood in the teeth of such weather. As the paws drew to a halt beside me, I opened my eyes and looked.

The darkest, saddest eyes I have ever seen gazed back into mine from their own level. They were set in a face of white fur that edged into a neat trimming of dark gray about the cat-like lower jaw, the neatly pointed ears, and the flattish muzzle. White fur covered the rest of the shape, which consisted of a compact and short-tailed body set high upon slender, oddly-jointed legs. A strange beast, altogether, unlike any in the books that I had studied so painstakingly at School.

There was no feeling of ill about it. It stood patiently while I studied it. When I began to sing it, it made a strange sound, a thrumming that just missed being a purr. And the shape I limned on the inside of my mind was no beast at all. Still it was not of my kind, either. And it was misted over, as if the gods wished its true shape concealed. But it was clear that a thinking being stood at my side in that ensorcelled wood.

# 5

## The House in the Lake

WE stood for a time, that creature and I, feeling one another with senses that few living beings possess. I almost forgot its shape, marveling at the spirit that dwelled within. The sadness that looked forth from its eyes came from its depths . . . some old sorrow lay inside the Winter Beast, though it was now pushed to the back by a new interest. For it had taken upon itself a task.

So much I could learn from my singing and my sensing. That I was the task and at least a part of the interest, I felt fairly sure. But its purposes were unfathomable to my arts. I waited upon its will.

The forest was again snapping and crashing about us, and patters of ice struck my face when some nearby branch bounded through its companions to shatter on the frozen ground. I felt certain of one thing: a clear space was much to be desired.

As if my thought spurred it to action, the Beast turned with the grace of a dancer and moved away into the wood from which I had come. It looked back and bowed its head, and I moved after it, careful of my footing but glad to have a guide, however strange. When it was satisfied that I followed and that its gait was not too swift for me, it flowed almost silently through a wood that was now catching the first rays of sunlight on a brilliant, cold morning.

I walked with half my attention on my guide and the other half directed upward. As the sun rose higher, the forest became a place enhanced with light and music. If the crystal sculptures that had intrigued my child-self at School had been endowed with the chiming of elfin musics, they might have dimly approximated that forest. The constant tinkling and shattering of ice against ice, the eye-piercing dazzle of light refracted through and reflected from ice on all sides and above and below almost dizzied the mind.

Once I found that I had stopped. The Beast had returned to my side, waiting patiently while I finished my rapt gazing into the miracle about me. When I looked down into those dark eyes, a glint of something sparked there for a moment. I almost believed it to be laughter.

With a sigh of pure joy, I took up my role as follower. The Beast set her pace slowly enough so that I could admire the magics and walk at the same time. So we went among the trees, taking the more open ways and avoiding the overhanging branches as much as might be. The day wore to noon, and still the forest endured, though the layering of ice grew thinner and less all-encompassing, as if only the hem of the storm had touched these more distant regions. We stopped, after a long while, and I ate from my store. The Beast nodded to me solemnly and slipped into the trees. I knew that she was after food for herself, and I waited for her as she had done for me.

When she returned, she set a sharper pace. On this less icy ground I held my own, and we moved rapidly through a younger wood than that we had left. There were glades, now, and thickets of young trees, unshadowed by somber roofs of mang. Fewer really huge trees were to be seen, and those stood alone in clearings of their own making.

The last light was touching the lightly iced tips of the tallest trees when we emerged from the edge of the wood and found ourselves beside a still black lake that was as smooth as a mirror with no ripple to be seen upon its surface. When we came near to its edge, I saw that it was frozen, though its deeps were clear. I had never seen ice so still and flawless and transparent. I bent to look. As I did, the Winter Beast touched my shoulder with one of her padded paws.

From where we stood, we could see the distant shore with its upthrusting trees. As the last of the light glimmered away from the western sky and the first chilly stars winked into being above us to reflect in the lake, something began to fog into being. At the center of that frozen lake, something was coming into view.

The faraway trees disappeared. The bulk of something tall and large loomed against the sky. I could now see, silhouetted by stars, a squat tower rising above a domed structure.

Foreboding filled me . . . the urge to turn my steps away and to seek no more in that spectral place. I closed my eyes, and a niggle of the Power touched me like a goad. "What place is this you have brought me to?" I asked the Beast.

She gazed at me sadly, her eyes trying to say what her lips could not. Then she set her paw on my shoulder and gave me a tiny push toward the tower. She was so intent upon making me see what she wished me to do that she was panting with the effort.

Suddenly my intuitions woke from their daze, and I said, "There, I take it, is the spot from which my troubles came? There sits the mind that imposed its thought and its spell upon the innocent forest where I slept?"

She sighed and sat on her haunches, her silvery whiskers twitching in the starlight like filaments of light. Nodding slowly, she gazed toward the tower that now stood, black and solid, against the sky. As I followed her gaze, I saw a light blink on in the upper reaches of it. No warm glow of lamp or hearthfire, it was like the radiance of a cold blue star, lost in untenanted space. It spoke of no being with the needs and emotions of men. There was no comfort in it for body or mind or spirit.

I shuddered. "Must we go out to that unchancy place?" I asked the Beast, and she thrummed her odd purr and rose to her feet.

We set our feet upon the ice with caution verging on despair. The Beast, though determined on this course, was patently not happy at the thought of carrying it through, though she led the way, stopping to guide me around any spot that felt unsafe to her sensitive paws.

We moved quite silently. The stars blazed down—and up— at us from sky and lake; the light in the window burned coldly before us. The feeling grew in me that I was entering another state of being from that one I had always known.

It was a longer journey than it had looked. Those staring stars had arced a quarter-way across the heavens before we came under the dark wall of the keep. There were no guard walls, no iron-studded gate. The lake must have served as sufficient protection to the builders. What foe would essay a winter campaign in weather so frigid that the lake froze to its bottom? Only a mad Singer and a Winter Beast might make such a foray.

We found a step that led into a flight of stairs that curved upward, following the swell of the tower's shape to a door that was set into the thick wall. That door was fastened with a simple latch. Surely, the tenant of this keep was unworried for his safety. I pressed the handle, the latch lifted, and the Beast and I walked cautiously into the dark well that was the shaft of the tower. Only a sliver of that cold blue light, shining on the wall above, told us that our quarry must still be in his place.

The Beast was catlike in more than one way. She made her way up those close-set, railless steps with the certainty of one who goes in full day. She made no sound, and I, trained in all the ways of the Singers, had learned also to walk silently on any surface. Only the hollow sound of water dripping far below us broke the stillness, and I found time to wonder how it could remain unfrozen in so terribly cold a place.

However, most of my attention was centered in my boot soles, as I set them carefully on those ice-rimed steps, steadying myself with one hand against the rough and chilly stone of the wall on my left. So we rose up into the tower, not swiftly but not slowly: cautiously, but with awful recklessness. And as we went up, I felt an oppression, as though I were climbing into a cloud of ill thoughts and evil deeds.

The Beast, too, felt the atmosphere of the place, for she paused, now and again, and waited for me to set my hand on her back. Then, as if comforted, she would go on again.

We came to the top at last. There we emerged through an opening into a floored place where a corridor curved sharply to the right, then the left, as if it followed the tower's wall. Before us was a door, heavy and well made, but open a crack. Thence had come the sliver of light that we had followed.

Without touching that portal, we peeped through the opening, the Beast lowering her head so that I might see through above it. The room beyond was brilliant with light, the blue radiance dancing upon walls that seemed made of diamond—or ice. My breath fogged thickly in the deeper chill that flowed from the chamber. I put my hand before my nose, that the mist of my breath might not enter the room and be seen before we were ready to announce our presence.

I could see, in my narrow angle of vision, the corner of a table. There seemed to be a sort of webbing of silvery thread set into a wooden frame. I moved a bit to change my angle in order to see better. Then I froze into the stillness of anger. The webbing was anchored on its four corners to posts made to resemble mang trees. Those trees hung thick with icicles.

The web was a demented tangle of loops and whorls and

interlocking knots. In its middle hung a doll. I was too far away to determine its features, but on its diminutive feet were russet boots.

What mischievous mind had woven its sick spell over the clean and ancient wood? I reached forward and pushed the door inward. It swung against the wall with a thud, and the figure that had been hunched over the webwork straightened in surprise.

We went in, the Beast and I, as calmly as if we were visiting a familiar haunt. Once inside, I closed the door and set its bar into the slots, for I had no knowledge of what companions my host might have that might come behind us. Then the Beast moved to the left and sat against the wall, curving her short tail around her paws. I went to the right and set my back to the stone beside the window that we had seen from afar.

The being that stood between us was no sort that had ever come to being on my world. It was over-tall, thin to wispiness. Chill gray fabric covered chill gray flesh that bore no hue of the life we know. Its face was long and narrow, with a high-bridged nose that began above its brow. Slitted eyesockets held within them a kind of focus of mist, also gray.

That mist was now shot with cold lightnings as the creature bent it upon me. A voice that the north wind might have envied said, "How come you here, Singer? You are enmeshed in my trap, which should hold you from the rash purposes that rasped against my attention. My devices sensed your coming, and I knew that I must detain you. You could not escape from my weaving!"

"You see me," I replied. "I do not know your kind, but you evidently know little of Singers. We are the servants of the gods."

"The gods!" he whispered, and a laugh like the breaking of a raw branch in the wind shook him. "We of Ethras know no gods, only our own . . . amusements. It has been long since

I interfered with the concerns of the primitives of Tyrnos. I have watched you evolve from brutes of the forest, though only a short span of my life has been lived on this forsaken world. It has been my pleasure, from time to time, to meddle in your affairs. I must admit that I draw much refreshment from the struggles of those whom I take in my toils." Then his tone of musing vanished. "Yet none have ever escaped me! You cannot stand in this tower!"

"Here I stand," I answered. "Your webs are nothing to the Power that the gods have entrusted to me and my kind. It brought to me the Winter Beast, who sits by yonder wall washing her whiskers and waiting. She led me to you. Now I stand here and ask you—who among my folk are grown so self-indulgent and so vain, so reckless of the duties of power that they allow you to exist and to prey upon their own folk? What reason have you to wish to halt my purpose, unless you protect those whom I am going to observe?"

He laughed again, and I felt my muscles twitch with pain at the unbearable humorlessness of that sound. A twinge of doubt niggled at me. How could I, if what he said was true, defy one who had existed before my own race began? What stores of knowledge, what other and more potent sorceries might he unleash upon me?

I almost faltered, but the Winter Beast rose to her feet, lashed her short and furry tail, and spat a derisive comment at the gray one. My spirits rose instantly. The gods had sent her to me. The gods had guided me to him. They would not contrive so if my task were hopeless.

I thrust my heels against the floor, set my head straight upon my spine, and looked into those not-eyes. "You will not answer my questions? Even though they are asked at the direction of the gods?" I queried, though I already knew the answer. "You will seek to play with me the wicked games you used with my ignorant forebears?" A thought came to me, and I voiced it. "Are you not, I wonder, of the very race that foments wickedness in Tyrnos? Does your thought run even to Raz . . . and to the Citadel?"

It laughed. "There are more of my kind upon this mudball than one, Singer. All have their own interests and purposes. We do not interfere, one with the other. But sometimes we aid, when it suits our whim."

I nodded. Then I drew a deep breath and felt the Power drawing into my bones, my nerves, and my lungs. I sang.

I sang a soul so alien that I was chilled, even as I sang. Voids in cold spaces seemed to surround me; worlds deserted, worlds never tenanted, worlds destroyed spun through my mind. I sang an outcast, warped and wicked and driven away, with others of his ilk, from his own place by his own people. I sang a spirit so obdurate in its loneliness that it shunned the chance for companioning. I sang a being that had no place upon Riahith.

When my voice first burst into the frozen room, the being laughed yet again. When my song took shape, it started, then stilled. And when the shape that was its soul hung against the polished ice of the wall, it stared at it as though it had forgotten my existence.

I fell silent, the Power still thrumming along my fibers. Now the gods held that being in their hands, winnowing him in the wind that was their will. He twisted in their grasp, those strange eyes sparkling their lightnings into the nothingness about him. He seemed to grow even thinner, until only a flimsy gray robe struggled in the cold air.

There was a terrible sigh, and the robe fell to the floor, empty of its wearer. I had an instant's vision of a bereft soul, bodiless, powerless, fleeing away into the spaces between the stars. Pain moved through me. The Beast brought me to myself, rubbing her head against my cloak.

When she was certain I had returned to myself, she stared toward the window. Morning had come. The lake below the window was alive with pinkish light. The sun was beginning to touch the high clouds to gold, and the tower felt warmer than it had. I looked across toward the circling wood—but no wood was there, only sparkling mists.

As the sun reached into that east window, I carefully began to unwind the snare, beginning at one post and untangling the thread as I went. I did not dare to cut or to break through that weft. Though the departure of the Ethran might have broken the spell, I had no assurance that it was so. My only course was to unmake it, as nearly as could be done, in the way that it had been made.

As I worked, the icicles on the tiny mang trees began to drip. I rolled the silvery thread into balls, tying each off neatly as it was completed. When the doll was freed, I left the rest to make a web of brightness in the newborn sunlight.

My eyes were heavy with sleep; weariness rolled over me, now that I had no task at hand. The Beast, too, yawned a wide pink yawn. We looked about the tower. It was now almost warm. The brightness that glossed the walls had gone —melted or dissolved with the dissolution of the master of the place.

I spread the fur cloak in a corner formed by some shelving and lay down. The Beast watched me interestedly as I rolled myself securely in those warm folds. Then she lay beside me, her furry body lending its heat to my own. As the sun moved up the east, the Winter Beast closed her eyes, and I followed suit. We fell immediately into secure and dreamless sleep.

# 6

## *Lisaux of the Black Shield*

WE woke late, as the last of the sunlight was dying in the sky. Rising, we went forth from the tower to stand beside the domed house that rose beside it. I have been asked, in days since, why I entered that forbidding place, after my struggle with the Ethran. I can only reply that it never occurred to me not to enter it. Any structure on that eery islet must contain evidence of the alien's activities. Those activities, I felt with deep certainty, were closely concerned with the questions that spurred me on toward the Citadel.

It was not, however, an easy place to enter. Formed of some grayish stone that fitted together so cleverly that a hair might not have slipped into the cracks between its blocks, it curved upward in a half-sphere as smooth as that of a bubble on the water. We could see no door, no window, no skylight or other opening. Still, I knew that it must have one, if we could only learn the secret. As the starlight blazed down upon the lake at our backs, I thought to sing it.

It is a weird thing to sing a structure. It is even stranger to sing one built by nonhuman hands. As I sang, tensions wove through me and the air about me. I saw the big stone blocks float effortlessly in the air above the lake, coming to rest exactly as they now lay in the wall. I felt a shadow of that controlling will that had been the Ethran, shaping, moving, arranging all to its satisfaction.

I watched the stones fall into position—and I saw the place where no stone fell, though the semblance of stone was placed there. Touching the Beast, I went forward again and walked through what seemed to be solid masonry, into the house beyond.

It was cut into a maze of winding passageways and small rooms that were furnished with mechanisms and shapes of wood and fabric that were unrecognizable to me. The outward corridor followed the curved wall of the dome, the doors of the rooms and the mouths of the cross-passages opening into it. I went slowly along, opening doors to any chambers that were closed, though few were. All seemed empty, except for strange machineries. No sound except our own breathing and the clicks of the doors moved in all the place.

I marked the first door, opposite to the entryway, with a thread from one of the silvery balls that had gone into my pouch. When I came again to that spot, I nodded to the Beast, who blinked solemnly back. We turned, with one accord, down the first of the corridors leading into the depths of the building.

That was a stranger journey, almost, than any I have ever made. Delusions had been built into the fabric of the structure. Some were visible ones: beasts that roared and grimaced, seemingly solid flesh, in the middle of the corridor; armored warriors that threatened with lance and sword. But I had been trained to pierce delusion and illusion, and these posed no problem. The Beast seemed, also, to recognize their unreality.

As we progressed along that drunkenly winding way, another sort of spell found us. It was a subtler thing, beginning as a shiver along the bones, a tingling of nerves. Apprehension began to raise my neck hair and pinch goose pimples into my skin. The Beast, too, was twitching her whiskers and shaking her head as if something were troubling her mightily. We closed ranks, taking comfort in the warmth of solid flesh against solid flesh.

Then fear came. It had no reason, no logic. It differed from anything I had found in the self of the Ethran, and I knew that another entity dwelled within that round house.

Blind panic had been set to run free in that corridor, and it was a terrible thing to do battle with. We stopped, the Beast and I, and set our backs together, she sitting on her haunches, I standing as straight as my training taught me I must. The fear beat down upon us like a driving rain of summer, drenching us in our own sweat, even in the cold of that untoward place.

I opened my mouth to sing, but my throat was frozen with terror. No voice was there with which to sing. Still, I felt the Power beginning its coursing through my body. As if she knew my problem, the Beast turned and thrust her furry side against me, feeling, I believe, the Power through me. She opened her white-fanged mouth, and her voice cried through the halls.

She did not sing as do Singers. No picture followed the wavering notes that her shrill voice sounded. But the fear began to die. She drew Power from me, interpreted it through her own incomprehensible self, and patterned her own song from it. From deep purr-notes to ear-splitting screeches, she shook the fear loose from the walls and the stone and quenched it in the moiling sea of her music. When she stopped, she turned and rubbed her head against me, as if in apology.

"Thank you," I said. "You did what I could not do, my friend, and I am grateful to you."

Before we could move from the spot, a despairing yell came from the dark depths before us. The light that had glowed in the outer corridors seemed to die away gradually as we penetrated deeper into the building, so I took from my pack the lightglass that all Singers carry and spun its wheel to light it. In that steady circle of brightness, we went onward, seeking the source of that cry.

The Beast's song seemed to have exorcised the spells that the house had held, for we were beset no more. It was as well, for the intricate passageways converged at one point, and we were hard put to choose a direction. The Beast, with her keener senses, indicated the right, at last, and we set off down a way that seemed to be straighter than any we had seen so far.

It grew darker and darker yet, as if there had been unseen skylights or other light sources in the ways we had followed that were now being left behind. My lightglass shone steadily as a star. Flickers of shiny stuff caught its brightness and sparked in the stuff of the walls. We found our way quickly, then faster still, as if some urgency were upon us.

Another cry from the deeps before us spurred us to even greater efforts. We flew down that hall like two gusts of wind. When we emerged from it, we found ourselves in the heart of that strange house.

We stood beneath the central curvature of the dome. The round chamber was large, and as we entered it, illumination blossomed inside the walls, making it clear that this was the heart of the mysterious activities of the Ethran, as well as that of the house. Head-high screens partitioned the room, but it soared above them, making them seem insignificant.

Yet as we stood, gaping upward into that great space, we heard, near at hand, a despairing groan that died away with the waxing of the light. Without glancing again at the chamber, I began opening doors in partitions. If the outer rooms had contained strange machineries, these cubicles were filled with things that none, I guessed, of my kind had ever seen— or wanted to see. Their uses were as unguessable as their construction, yet there was a dire feel to them that hinted of terrible functions presided over by even more terrible beings.

There were spaces filled with nothing except gray mists that roiled gently at the opening of the door. There were spaces filled, literally, with space—a nothingness that blurred away the walls of the room and would have sucked my consciousness into some obliterating vortex, if I had not looked away very quickly. There were rooms filled with an intricacy of silvery webbing, much like the miniature maze in the tower.

In one of those we found our man. He hung, caught in the web, like a fly in a spider's trap, or like the doll that had hung in that smaller weaving that I had unmade. Yet there was a difference. This was no silvery thread, easily untangled and unwound. The man was caught in a complex of silver light that wound, contrary to the way of any other rays I had ever seen, into circling knots and curving snares. About the entire mesh prickled an aura of hostility that made me pause.

Now the overhead light reached its maximum brightness and steadied into brilliance, and I turned out the lightglass and stood back to consider the problem we faced. Strangely, though the air itself seemed to glow, those silver strands shone strongly, marking themselves plainly upon the lambent air.

In their midst, the man was still, his mouth tightly closed, as if against pain. His eyes, too, were shut. I thought that he had only limited consciousness. It was likely that the weird timbres of the Beast's singing had pierced the half-stupor in which he existed, rousing him to cry out. Well for him that they had, or we might not have searched so diligently for him.

He was clad in black leather and black-enamelled steel. Though he was not in full armor, his corselet had been left to him, as well as his helm. Its visor had been removed and lay on the floor beneath him. A black blade leaned in a corner like a tidy wife's broom, its sling and scabbard in a limp huddle beside it. On his dangling feet, shiny leather caught the light in sullen streaks.

He was not ill-looking at all, though his pale face was tight and grim. I had seen such a look before, in my early years of training. One who had been the captive of a sorcerer had come to us for healing. I well remembered the torments that I had helped to sing out of his soul.

Angered by the recollection, I looked closely at the sides of the small chamber. The light must have its source there, for it seemed to run, as well as the puzzled eye could tell, horizontally, more than vertically. The pebbly texture of the wall told me little, and I knew that I dared not go amid those treacherous beams to feel for openings.

I could see no usefulness in singing that alien thing. I stood there and drew upon the Power, drawing my breath deeply, as if for song; then, as the still-active tensions built again, I tried to focus them into my vision, rather than into my throat. The augmenting energies shook me with their force. My teeth clacked together, my elbows trembled against my sides. Rigors rippled down my muscles.

The place blurred around me, as I felt my eyes straining with a vision other than my own. Then I saw.

The light was a living being. Not a device, as I had thought, nor a remnant of the Ethran's strange power, but a creature! I opened my mouth, and the dammed-up force within me burst forth in an ascending crescendo of notes so powerful that they almost tore the tissues of my throat. Under that assault, the walls of the cubicle shattered into fragments. The black sword fell to the floor, as the web of light writhed and sidled, still holding its victim. It was, quite obviously, trying to elude the potencies focused upon it.

I closed my eyes and sang, trusting to the gods to tend the man in the web. When the power began to ebb, I opened them again, in time to see the black figure fall to the floor with a clang. The bright shape flickered and was gone.

The Beast was already beside the man, who had fallen on his back. I knelt beside him and removed his helm. That caught on something behind him, and I discovered that he wore, tied to his back, his shield, also black but worked in gold with an ornate symbol. Relieving him of both, I loosed his leather garment at the neck and touched his forehead to find if he were fevered.

With that touch, he opened his eyes and looked up at me uncomprehendingly for a moment. Then he struggled to sit, and I helped him. We all remained as we were for a time, studying one another. I was kneeling, the Beast sitting on her haunches with her short tail straight out behind her, and the man sitting flat, his hand on his shield.

Something moved among us. The Powers that had used the place so short a time before had left some emanation that allowed even fallible mortals to feel the truths of one another directly and without doubt. We were, in our exceeding differences, much the same at heart. So the man and I smiled, and the Beast purred her deep note.

Then I rose, and the man struggled to his feet, though his limbs wavered under him.

"How long were you caught, yonder?" I asked him.

"Time, Lady, did not exist . . . there," he said. "It was late summer when I came through the forest on the track of my own Lady's abductors. The road dissolved before my eyes, leaving me bewildered among trees that stretched on either hand forever. I wandered for days."

He looked at me with puzzlement in his honest eyes. "I, Lisaux, hunter and tracker, as well as warrior, was lost in a forest. It fogs the mind to think on it." Then he remembered that we had not made our names known in a formal fashion. He colored at his own forgetfulness.

"I am known as Lisaux of the Black Shield, holder of the Fiefdom of the Noble Shepherds in Malchion. Who may you be, Lady?"

"I am a Singer of Souls," I answered, "and we do not claim names in the manner of other folk. You may call me Singer, and that will do well enough."

"I have heard tales of the Singers of Tyrnos," he answered. "In the southeast of Malchion, among the tall peaks where I make my home, we welcome wanderers with tales to liven the shut-away winter days and nights. While the north wind made her song outside our door, Leeana and I heard a minstrel sing of the Singers. A strange song . . . one to intrigue the mind. Do you truly sing virtue into the rulers of Tyrnos?"

"Not we, but the Power of the gods, working through us," I said. "We go about all the lands, singing in every noble hall and house. We work also among the commons, healing inner ills that injure the mind and the spirit. I have even comforted a cow that mourned for her lost calf. We are no awesome folk, we Singers. Rather we are simple, poorly clad, giving ear to all we meet.

"I am not wandering in the usual fashion of my kind, however. It has come to my mind that there is rot at the very root of Tyrnos. I make my way south to see the truth, if it may be done."

He laughed, a hoarse grunt with more of pain than joy in it.

"Well may you suspect such," he said. "My Lady was brought into Tyrnos. She was taken from me in the spring, while I was among the herds that moved back to the high pastures. When I returned to our home, she had been gone for a day and a night. Hasten though I might, I could not catch up to those brigands who broke down our door and carried her from her home, bound and stricken senseless, according to the servants.

"I have taken up arms again, though I forsook war for the life of my sires, among the sheep of our holding, when I wed Leeana. Only the black blade can cut deeply enough into the flesh of those who have injured her. I have followed into Tyrnos, never knowing if she still lives, to find and slay those who have taken her from me." His voice broke, and tears rose into his pale eyes, rolling down his cheeks without shame or hindrance.

I felt a rush of hotness rise into my chest. The land that I had been taught to revere, to love, and to keep cleansed of wickedness was polluted, it began to seem, by some fearful miasma. All my training rebelled against the thought of such vileness. My heart was touched, also, at the grief of Lisaux, who stood with tears on his cheeks, asking nothing of me.

"Though I have not the power of seeking," I told him, "I will come with you, and we two will search out all Tyrnos, if need be, from the mountains to the sea. If she lives, your Leeana will be found. If not, we will find those who slew her. What a Singer can do, I will do, and that is no small count of Powers."

Before he could answer, the Beast rose and came between us, looking into my eyes, then into his, as if trying without words to convey to us some thought. I had known that she was a thinking being, but it is so easy to let our minds be deceived by appearances that I had given no thought to her reactions to Lisaux's story. Now it came to me, and I was borne up with excitement.

"She is saying that her senses are acute, her eyes and ears and nose more sensitive than ours. She, of all of us, can find Leeana, if only you have some possession of hers about you that may give the Beast her scent!" I exclaimed.

Lisaux put his hand into the front of his leather garment and drew forth a silken sleeve, edged with lace. "They took her by force from the house," he said, "and her sleeve was caught and torn away by a servant who tried to aid her. I have brought it all this way, simply that I might have something of hers about me to bear me company." He held it toward the Winter Beast. She inhaled deeply, her nose buried in the frail wisp.

She looked into my eyes, and I looked, in turn, up at Lisaux. "Now we will find Leeana," I told him.

# 7

## *To Search Amid the Snow*

WE left the house, as we had entered it, by starlight. I think that it might not have been possible to leave it, once inside, in any other way. By day it seemed, to my trained manner of thinking, that it must exist in some dimension other than that of Riahith. Its gradual appearance with the coming of darkness seemed to be a clue to that. The fact that we had seen a lake glittering in the morning sunlight did not prove that the lake under our feet was the one we had seen from the tower window.

Though still solid enough to walk upon, the ice seemed to be beginning to melt, for a thin slish of water slopped about our steps. The tree-stitched edge of the lake ahead of us was mirrored, together with the staring stars, in a liquid film that rippled faintly with the breeze and our movements.

I, for one, was glad enough to set my feet upon honest soil again. The Beast, too, hopped onto the shore with a wag of her tail that bespoke enthusiasm. Only Lisaux seemed indifferent, and I felt that he was still in a partial daze, after his long captivity.

The ice had all but melted from the trees, the starshine catching only an occasional sparkle. The breeze, though cuttingly chill, hadn't the vicious edge that the earlier wind had possessed. There was still a rime of ice underfoot, and I noticed that the Beast was examining it with close attention.

Not until we reached a spot that was totally clear of frost did I realize her true situation. She was, in a literal sense, a Winter Beast. Where the ice ran, she could run. Where it stopped, she must come to a halt. When I looked deep into her eyes and asked her the direct question, her thrumming purr acknowledged that this was true.

I looked at her, shining there in the cold starlight, and I knew that she must be set free to wander over Tyrnos, if ever Lisaux might regain his lady.

"I shall sing snow," I said to her.

Her purr grew louder, and Lisaux woke from his daze with a grunt.

"Snow will hinder us!" he protested. "Snow covers tracks and hides trails and chills the seeker to the bone."

"The trail you followed is long buried in the debris of days and weeks gone by," I said to him. "Only the Beast can winnow out, from all the rest, whatever scent is left of Leeana. She can go only as far as the white arm of winter reaches. Ice is treacherous underfoot and dangerous overhead. But snow . . . snow will give her mobility without hindering us overmuch. I shall sing snow."

He accepted the finality of my answer, and I walked away under the young mang trees that grew beside the lake. There I breathed deeply, felt the Power begin its pulsing along my veins. Then I shaped that Power . . . differently. Instead of directing it into a being or a thing, I fanned it outward from me toward the sky that glittered with hard white stars against a hard black background. With it all, I thought snow, felt snow, smelled snow.

The wind changed as I sang. I felt the chill breeze whip about to northward and become a bladelike wind. When I opened my eyes, a thin wisp of high cloud was edging over the horizon.

I turned to my companions. "Let us sleep now," I said. "When we wake, if the gods will it, we will awaken to snowfall."

Though so lately brought from his sleeplike state, Lisaux made no protest. As for the Beast and me, we had labored long since our rest in the tower. We huddled together against a tree. My capacious fur cloak wrapped about us all three, with room to spare, and in warmth and companionship, we fell gently asleep.

Dawnlight woke us, aided by a rush of biting wind. A spatter of driven flakes touched my cheek as I peered out above the robe. Then I touched the Beast and pointed upward. Her dark eyes regarded the gray batts of rolling cloud with satisfaction, and she, in turn, nudged Lisaux. He groaned awake, looked upward, then turned respectful eyes upon me.

"I did nothing but call upon the gods." I laughed, struggling from the cocoon of fur. "Give your regard to them, for they have weighed our cause and our need in the balance of their judgment, and they have found us worthy of their help. For that one thing give thanks, Lisaux. It may be the first step in regaining your Leeana."

We ate from my pouch, standing in the thickening snow, while the Beast stole away into the forest to find her own repast. When she returned, we set out with the dawn at our backs and the snow-laden wind on our right cheeks. Of necessity, we followed the Beast. Lisaux trod closely behind her, and I brought up the rear, watching for any sign of the road I had traveled into this immense wood.

There was no road. The Beast had led me eastward in bringing me to the house in the lake. We went away from it westward. If the road had existed, we must certainly have crossed it, soon or late. I was left to realize that I had walked the Ethran's snare for many leagues. Some strand of the silver thread in my pocket had marked out a counterfeit way for my feet to follow.

The thought made me shudder. If a Singer of Tyrnos might be so easily misled, what hope was there for the others, high and low alike, who lacked the training and the talent for calling directly upon the gods for aid?

The world curdled about us in a cloud of white. We went forward, now, treading closely, toe to heel. I reached, now and again, to touch Lisaux's black cloak, for it all but disappeared in the dizziest swirls that caught us in their grasp. The Beast led without hesitation, and we followed with the blind trust that was all that was left to us. Alone in the storm, without her guidance, we would have staggered in circles until we died.

Twice we stopped to rest in hollows that the Beast found in thick-boled mang trees. We ate a bit, hoarding my diminished store of food, and sipped from my bottle before we fell into exhausted sleep. When we woke the second time, the snow had stilled to an occasional wayward flake, though the sky was still and white and low-hung with more cloud.

Climbing stiffly from our burrow, we looked about and realized that the wood was thinning. At the edge of vision was a glare of unbroken white that spoke of grassland ahead, or of fields. As we looked, the Beast flung up her head, her whiskers twitching, and opened her mouth in a soft hiss of excitement.

"Do you have the scent?" I asked her. Her ears flipped forward and back, forward and back, as if in reply.

Lisaux caught my hand. "Let us hurry," he cried. "I was following westward when I was caught in the warlock's snare. The keep where the villains hide must be there . . ." and he waved his free hand toward the lands ahead of us.

Hurry we did, through the last of the forest, crunching through the knee-deep snow. When we emerged from the hem of the wood into the wide lands, we stood stunned at the scene before us.

We were near the edge of an escarpment. About us, the

land was flat as a plate and glaring with snow. The meadows before us seemed to have been gashed with a gigantic cleaver. Where the edge fell away, we could see for leagues out over the sunken lands. They, too, were cloaked with white.

Walking forward, we found ourselves looking down a terrible declivity that seemed, in the white light, to be straight and unbroken. However, when we examined it closely we could see that it was marked with fissures and ledges, giving us hope that it might be negotiated.

The Winter Beast showed less interest than we two-footed ones in the cliff. Her great eyes scanned afar, while we sought for a path downward. Before we found what we were seeking, she gave a low growl that brought us to her side. When we followed her gaze, we saw a curl of smoke, off to the left. The stack that emitted that smoke was down over the curve of the rolling plain below, but the telltale sign upon the air was all we needed.

Though I had never seen the Sunken Plain, I knew its history and geography. It was sparsely populated, only three families holding the leagues of grassland in fief. Each of those had chosen to build a keep to house their folk, for the Plain was a wild and wanton place, crossed frequently by brigands who fled from the Citadel northward, or from Malchion, or even Ageron.

All of those families—Holdorn, Garloek, and Endeor—were stout and honest ones, blessed with many children and good repute. I wondered, gazing after that smoke trail, if a tragedy like the one that had overtaken the household of Kalir had now wiped one of these from the face of Tyrnos. It would suit me ill if the henchmen of the Ethran and his ilk now sat at ease before the hearth of a murdered clan.

Now we sought in earnest for a way to reach the bottom of that cliff. To follow its edge until it met the rising lands to the north would take days that we could not afford to lose. At all risk, we must find footholds enough to go down here.

The Beast discovered the cut. It angled downward between two flat boulders that overhung that dizzy edge by an arm's length. Below it was another flat rock, much like a step set into the face of the cliff. Though Lisaux protested, I let myself down into the slot, knowing that my lesser weight and bulk might make the difference in getting out again, if the way should prove to be impassable. When I had made him realize that he could easily pull me back, while I would find much difficulty in doing the same for him, he nodded grimly and agreed.

It was dizzy work. Once I was out on the face of the rock, however, I could see more easily the irregularities below me and to either side. There were crevices and ledges, and by good fortune (or the gods' clever design), this westward-facing cliff had been only lightly dusted with the snow that had blown so brisky from due north. This made my task much lighter, for I had only to pause now and again to brush away shallow drifts in order to see what lay beneath.

A few ells down, I felt confident enough of the passage to call to Lisaux and the Beast. Then we moved together, though separated by goodly distances, down that steep scarp.

It was well that we moved almost as much to one side or the other as directly downward, else the falling of pebbles and snow and larger stones might have dislodged me or Lisaux. As it was, seldom were we in straight line, up and down, in our zigzagging way, and chance falls of rock were left to clatter their way harmlessly past.

The wind, which had all but died away in the night, now began to rise into a gale. Our chilled hands slid on holds they were barely able to grasp. Our feet grew numb inside our boots. The Beast watched us with anxiety, scampering with frustrating agility along ways we could not attempt in order to come near and examine our faces and hands and the path (inaccurate term!) that we followed. At last she took up the lead, with a peremptory yowl that we understood without difficulty. She had decided, I knew, that without her guidance we would not reach the end of the climb before darkness fell. We had toiled away the forenoon and much of the afternoon in our efforts, and night was approaching. To spend a night on that height was folly without measure. Sleep would relax our grips and send us crashing downward. Still, to try moving along those perilous ways in darkness broken only by the dim snowlight would be even more foolhardy.

So she led us down, that admirable Beast, and when we flagged she sang to us. That woke us to our duties in a moment, be assured. By the time we set our numb feet onto the solid ground at the foot of the cliff, only snow and starlight aided us, but day was not long departed. As if to bolster our faith and courage, just beside the point at which we came down, a considerable cavern was chewed into the stone by the teeth of many winters.

We scuttled into it and dropped into a heap of mingled fur and flesh, too weary even to try to eat or to drink. In our sleep, we made better accommodation, for I woke in a snug huddle with the Beast's warm fur against my cheek. My cloak was spread over us all, and the body heat of the Beast had soaked through me, soothing away some of the aching that the climb had caused. On her other side, Lisaux yawned loudly, and I sensed that he, too, had been wrapped in that restful warmth.

His voice broke the morning stillness. "Without this excellent being, we would have died in the night," he said quietly. "Weariness had sapped all the energies of my body, and yours also, I well know. We could never have warmed ourselves sufficiently, here where there is no fuel for even a small fire. Leeana would have lived, if she still does live, in anticipation of a rescue that would never come."

We struggled upright, moaning at the nip of cold against our abused bodies. We dug into my pack and ate a bit of the dried fruit and cheese that Meltha had put there so many days before. My water bottle furnished enough drink to make it palatable, but we knew that we must soon find fuel and melt snow for a fresh supply. Then we moved about the cavern, out of the wind's reach, bringing our bodies back into a serviceable state.

When we again dared the Plain, the wind had died away to a whisper. Snow was falling lightly, silently, softly as a dream. No glimpse of sun could we find, for the cloud seemed to rest upon the top of the height we had descended. The Beast lifted her head and sniffed the air. Then she purred her deep thrum and moved away at an angle to the wall behind us.

Sure that she had again picked up that telltale trace of smoke, we stepped in her track, as much as might be done when two feet try to follow in the steps of four. She was all but invisible in the white morning, her fur blending so well into the snowscape that one who stood near, not knowing she was by, could have looked directly at her without seeing that she was there.

Deep though the footing was, obscure as was the day, we moved swiftly across the Plain. In twelve paces, the escarpment disappeared into the softly swirling snow. Twelve paces after that, Lisaux or I would have been totally disoriented. But our guide knew where she must go, and she led us without hesitation.

We did not stop for food or for rest. The day wore on and on, and it might have been noon or late afternoon when we came, at last, against a stone wall that stood just higher than Lisaux's head. There the Beast stopped. She looked into my eyes, then into those of Lisaux. We both understood that she must reconnoitre, while we waited silently for her return.

I laid my hand upon her head. Lisaux did the same. Then he made a curving sign in the air above her and said, "May the gods be with you, friend."

She grunted softly and was gone.

66

While we waited, we rummaged about for twigs beneath a scraggly old thorntree that grew up and over the wall. We made our fire as though our existence depended upon its being arranged with total exactitude. But we did not light it to flame. We waited.

Night fell. It was not true night, for the snowfall had quieted, and the white glare underfoot lit the world with its strange illumination. The cold was like glass that had congealed about us. We leaned against one another with my cloak wrapped about us both, sharing what warmth we could muster. We even slept a bit, there in the shelter of the rough wall.

We woke suddenly and with a start. The Beast stood beside us, eery in the strange light, her fur shining softly and her eyes like pits of deepest night. She nodded briskly, and I was reminded of one of the teachers at the School for Singers. Just so had she announced to us, "Now *this* is what we must *do,* immediately!"

She looked at the fire pile and nodded again. Lisaux knelt and spun the wheel of my lightglass, moving the glass aside so that the sparks fell upon a fluff of tinder we had raveled from his cloak. With a soft glow, the thing ignited, and soon we all three crouched about that tiny fire. I held the bottle of snow close, and soon there was a pleasant sloshing when I moved it.

When the bottle was filled, and we had drunk deeply and eaten the last of Meltha's supplies, our guide carefully swiped pawfuls of snow over the blaze until no sign remained that fire had ever burned there. Then she crept cautiously around the corner of the wall. We followed as silently as if we, too, had been Winter Beasts.

The wall, as we found, surrounded orchards and gardens. It girded a large plot of land. Along the side we now followed, the snow had drifted almost neck-deep, so that we were forced to walk wide of it, but the Beast padded across the tops of the drifts as if she had no weight at all.

We came, at last, to a small door set into the thickness of the wall. It was latched, but the Beast sprang lightly up and over, and in a moment we heard a chunking sound as her paw fell upon the inner catch. Then Lisaux put his shoulder to the door and heaved it, inch by inch, inward.

It must have been years since any had used that way, for the soil of the garden beyond had drifted with rain and wind to a depth of some inches against the portal. Only Lisaux's strength was able to force that way. I would have been compelled to try climbing the wall, had I been alone. And I am not nearly invisible, as is the Beast, against the snow.

We stood in the shelter of the inner part of the wall. A tangle of dead and blackened vine overhung the recess in which we were, giving us a secure moment to survey the place into which we had come.

We were within an old-fashioned fort-garth, one well able, by its size, to sustain a beleaguered family for long periods with fresh and preserved foods. A mound of manure stood sentinel beside the wall, waiting for spring. Fruit trees and vines were espaliered against the wall, also, and leafless berry bushes were spaced at its foot. In the center of the garden plot, a well curb and sweep gave evidence of the thrift and forethought of the builder of the keep. No common peril of the wild would find this place at its mercies.

Beyond the garden was the house itself, its windows squares of warm light in the dark blue chill of the night. A shed for wood enclosed the door that led into the garden, and we slipped along the wall to the corner of the house. Then, crouching, we dashed for the angle formed by the junction of the shed with the house wall. A window cast orange glow onto the snow beside us, and we ventured to glance with one eye's width into the room.

A clanking of pots told us it must be a scullery or a kitchen.

Cautiously peeping in, I swept my gaze over the room. There was a wide hearth, its edges black with soot. The fire in it lit an array of cranes and hooks that told of its use in cookery. To either side were wooden settles of good design.

On them sat five men, three on one side, two on the other. They were slick and sleek and well-clad enough, but the look of them turned me cold. I ducked beneath the window, that I might scan the other side of the kitchen without exposing my peering face to any chance glance at the window.

Beside a steaming tub stood a woman of middle age. Her bright hair had fallen from its shapely knot in elf locks, and it was stuck to her neck with sweat. Hands that were brown and tough-looking were busy, awkwardly scrubbing greasy pots. Her back, toward me, was one stiff and unyielding protest.

As I watched, a boot sailed through the air to thump against that proud back, and a jeering voice said, "Proud, a'nt she? Ye'd think, now, that a time o' the boot an' the whip might make'n more biddable. But no, she'n find blades where no blades be, to carven our hides wi'. She'n put ill-maken in the food. T'wonder is, old Ruif hanna scragged her afore now. Saven only he must have her t'take care o' that still-faced piece we carried away from Malchion."

I ducked again, to come up beside Lisaux. In the orange light that danced back at us from the snow, his lips were tight, but his eyes held anger to match that in my own.

I held my lips near his ear and whispered, "This must be Holdorn Keep. Garloek is to northward of the Plain, and Endeor guards the westernmost reaches. That must be Mayanna, wife of the Holdorn. I dread to know what has become of her husband and her sons and her young daughter."

Lisaux bent to hiss in my own ear, "She will be freed from these vermin. Aye, and her folk, too, if they live. And Leeana. Not for nothing did I survive the Ethran's spell. Not for nothing did you and the Beast bring me forth. Lisaux of the Black Shield has, in his time, been a warrior to strike fear into the hearts of *men* and black terror into those of villains like these. As for their Ruif—whoever he may be, if he has kept her from these, he has earned a clean death from me. No more, but no less."

There in the dark corner, glowing eerily in the strange light, we looked eye into eye, and the Beast nudged between us. We contracted, then and there, to avenge the Holdorn, if no more, and to wipe Tyrnos clean of those who roistered within.

# 8

## Holdorn Keep

THOUGH it would have been the strategically wise thing to do, we did not mount our attack then and there. We were weary to the bone, with that dead and fumbling feeling that comes after long periods of pushing the body past its limits. Even the Beast moved with less than her ordinary litheness, and we knew that we must all have rest before facing those within the house, who were rested and well-fed.

It would have been folly to seek our rest in the cold that now bit down upon the Plain. We looked at one another, then at the rows of dark and silent windows of the upper rooms that faced into the safety of the garden. It was too early for ruffians to seek their rest. Only one lighted square broke the dark symmetry of the second floor. We surmised that that was the chamber that held Leeana. Without need of words, we looked upward toward the shed roof.

Lisaux, after a long glance, crouched. I mounted upon his back, reaching from there the carven finials that finished the top of the shed roof. I drew myself up and looked about for a stronger support. Against the wall, I could see a shadow that resolved itself into a stout hook of the sort used for handling logs too heavy for convenient carrying. Unhooking my belt, I hung the steel buckle on the bottommost prong of the hook and dropped the wide band of leather into Lisaux's hands.

In a moment, we stood together on the shed, for the Beast had leaped soundlessly up as soon as we were safely positioned. The windows were at shoulder height to my companion, and he gently touched the dark sash that fronted onto the roof. It was locked, but a bit of work with the slender black blade he carried brought forth a decisive click, and then the sash slid sidewise.

We went in as silently as thieves by night and closed the window behind us. The room in which we found ourselves was chill and damp, as if no fire had burned there in months. This suited us. We felt our way about until we knew the contours of the chamber, the situation of its furnishings well enough to navigate it soundlessly in the darkness. Then we gave thought to rest.

The low bed was wide, and musty blankets were neatly folded at its foot. With one accord, we removed our boots, massaged our half-frozen feet into something resembling life, and tumbled onto the bed. With the blankets, my cloak, and the Beast's warmth between us, we slept in forgotten comfort for several hours.

I woke to the song of wind and the soft spat of blown snow. The Beast's eyes were open, for I could see a faint twin gleam. Lisaux sighed and woke, too, and we got to our feet and flexed our stiff bodies into motion again.

Then we approached the window. Peering out, we could see that the orange light still glowed from the upper window, three rooms to the left of the one we occupied. The kitchen light was out, and no other window that we could see was lighted. I tiptoed to the right-hand wall and laid my ear against it. The hint of rough snores and mutters told of a sleeper there. The other wall gave no hint of any tenant in the room beyond it.

Again, we had no need of words. Slipping out, we dug our toes into the stone ledge that crossed beneath the line of windows and inched along. The Beast leaped from the top of the shed to the overhang of the roof just above us and followed along its edge. We passed the two darkened openings and approached the third, which shone with brightness. As we neared it, the Beast, just above the spot, hissed a quiet warning, and we paused where we were.

A mutter of talk now grew distinct enough for hearing. "I'Ghanosh n' Gheth!" came a low rumble of an oath that was none I had even heard. Lisaux, however, cocked his head as if both oath and voice were known to him.

"Arvil af Eruifal," he whispered. "I should have known when those below called him Ruif. Ill was the day when his sottish mother bore him to his cold and evil sire. He was neighbor to us, as mountain folk account neighbors. Not more than seven leagues separated our holdings." His breath hissed between his teeth, and I could feel his rage as heat against my exposed cheek.

"Listen," I cautioned. "What we learn may be of value. That was no voice of a man who has his desire."

Setting my cheek tight against the frame of the window, I angled my gaze into the room. I could see the hangings of a bed, one booted foot swinging impatiently into view and out beyond them. Very near, as if just beside the window, I could see a dark sleeve and a woman's hand that tapped gently, gently, on what must have been a table set just under the sill. The hand held a flash of brightness that stilled with her hand and became a wicked but slender blade.

"Rest while you may, af Eruifal," said a chill voice beyond the pane. "While I have my blade, you rest alone. I have sat here for night after night, and it pleases me far better than any bed that holds you in it. Only the hope of the coming of my husband has held it from my own heart, as you well know. One evening you will unlock this door and there will be none here to listen to your bombast or to despise your lack of wit and courage."

"Hold your peace!" came the voice from the bed. "I have had none since my own madness led me to take you from your home. I must make a show of mastering you, that my own men may not turn against me. I must endure your tongue, which makes your blade seem dull. I must keep constant watch upon that miserable woman, that you do not conspire with her against us all.

"Your wit, I would swear, gave her the will to try all her tricks against us. But for my caution, she'd have poisoned us all, herself included, simply to know us dead. As for the ceaseless number of knives that she conjures into her possession, I feel more and more that the two of you must do witchery to bring them from the thin air."

"Do you truly believe that I must enrage her against you?" asked that cool voice. "Where is her young daughter? Ravished and murdered and thrown away with the household garbage. Where is her smallest son? That question your henchman Garz can likely answer. But all of us heard the child's screams through that first long night after you came to the door with your knife across the throat of her daughter. Then she made the dreadful error of trusting your given word.

"She would have done well to tell you to cut deep and give the child a clean death. She would have done well to bar the door and wait you out, until her men came back from Garloek, however long that may take. Or to embrace death for herself and her son and have done with it.

"The day will come, af Eruifal, when those of Holdorn come over yonder rise to the north. Four with a just grievance and the hearts of men can sweep like scythes through six guilt-ridden wretches with the hearts of jackals." The voice fell silent.

The man on the bed made no answer, but the light was suddenly extinguished. With my nail, I scritched lightly against the glass. Only a carefully drawn but unnaturally deep breath answered. In a moment, there was a tiny click, and I knew that the window was now unfastened.

We waited for a time, until deep breathing from the deeps of the room told us that Ruif slept. Then we crept in, one by one, finding that Leeana had moved silently aside, to be out of our way. A whisper from Lisaux, and she struck alight the lamp so recently extinguished.

We stood about the bed, four strangely assorted beings, and the light brought Ruif to his senses. His eyes moved from the Beast to me to Lisaux to Leeana, and they were totally unbelieving. Some dream, he seemed to be assuring himself, had followed him into wakefulness.

Lisaux stood above him, blade drawn, and said, "For your crimes against my own and against Holdorn, you are hereby sentenced to death, by Warrior-Right, Sword-Right, and the right of vengeance." As the last word left his lips, he struck, and the head of Ruif lolled aside amid a gush of bright blood.

We stood there, and the shock of sudden death rolled away on all sides of us. Leeana swayed, and Lisaux caught her as she fell.

She was frail as silk web, small and slender and seemingly without strength. Her eyes, however, looked up at us in apology for the inadequacies of her body, and they were indomitable. I am not large, it is true, but I am tough as bog root, for all my lack of size. Leeana had no such toughness about her.

Worn to a wisp by her ordeals, she seemed almost transparent. I marveled, looking down at her where she leaned in a deep chair, that she had not only withstood but intimidated the great brown villain in the canopied bed. I felt, for a fleeting moment, a dim reflection of the fascination and frustration that had held him in check.

"How long." I mused aloud, "do you suppose Ruif plotted to seize your wife? How long did he look upon her from afar and covet the treasure in your house?"

Lisaux grunted. "Had I known, his life would have ended long ago."

Leeana laughed, a mere whisper, but a laugh. "He thought me some sort of magical mistress, full of wiles to tempt men! That strange mind of his had brooded across all those miles between his keep and our own, making tales about me that their inventor believed. Only twice had he ever seen me. The first time was when he was bidden to our wedding. The second—do you mind it, Lisaux?—was when he came to the Counting of the Stags, only two years ago. I sat at your side at the Last-Night Feasting, though I was not well and had to rise from my sickbed to do it.

"From those two innocent and impersonal meetings, he wove a fantasy that his decaying reason drove him to implement. Had it not been for Dreean, your horsemaster, I would have had no weapon to use against his madness. But Dreean came up behind them as they dragged me from our home, caught me by the sleeve, and put into my hand this sliver of steel."

"How did you conceal it?" asked Lisaux. "I know they must have searched you carefully for weapons."

She leaned her head back against the cushion of the chair and held out her left arm. "Do you see this scar? There was a slash there where a blade caught me while I struggled with them. I drove the knife down into it, under the skin but avoiding the inner parts. When they let me down for food and rest, I begged a bandage for my wound. They tied it up, and my blade was well-hidden, though the pain of it rode with me out of Malchion and half across Tyrnos to this spot.

"Then, truly, I had need of it. When they tricked and bullied their way into this keep, Ruif had me locked into this room. He came, that night, after the shrieks of the children of Holdorn had died away forever. I let him disarm, remove boots and breeches. Then I moved to his side, took his chin into my hand, and laid the blade across his throat. He smiled, as if I caressed him. When the blade made itself felt, his eyes grew round, and he gurgled deep in his throat. I looked down into those staring eyes and told him what must be—and what must not be—between us.

"I laid his outermost skin open, just enough so that he understood me well. Then I chanted a rune that my father's mother used when she cursed the wolves that tore our flock. He took it for true witchery, and I forced the belief into him that I was able, if driven to it, to steal away life from him and his followers. I took, also, Mayanna of Holdorn under my protection and thus saved her life, though I could not save her body from indignity." She sighed, and her eyes closed as if her energies were all but drained away.

I moved away to the bedside again. Ruif's sword, a thin, straight blade, sharp on point and two edges of the diamond-shaped blade, hung in its scabbard from a post. I took it in my hand and whipped it through the air, making a vicious hum.

We are not taught swordplay or any martial art in the Schools for Singers. Our gifts are of other sorts. But there are times for release of anger, for washing away wrongs in the tides of vengeance. No song would I sing tonight. The short span of my childhood at home, when my brothers had practiced in secret with me as their blade-partner, would have to suffice.

We looked about at one another. Lisaux made a protective gesture toward his wife, but she held up her hand. "I have guarded myself for these many months, unaided and alone. Now you are here with formidable companions. Go about your business, Lisaux, and give no thought for me. I have not endured for so long only to be overcome at last."

The Beast gave her deep purr and thrust her head into the

77

woman's lap, her short tail lashing in circles. Leeana laid her hand upon the Beast's head and stroked the snowy fur. Then the creature stood on her four legs and looked questioningly at the window.

Lisaux grunted. "Right, friend. You are a skilled tactician, I see, though mine is the battle craft taught by experience. Go out the window and keep watch over the door."

He looked down at Leeana. "How is the main entrance secured, love? This being a keep, I doubt it has but one door looking onto the Plain."

Her eyes lighted. "I have all that you need, from May-anna. The great door is seldom opened to its full extent, though its outer leaves can be swung wide to admit carts and horses in time of peril. These are fastened with iron rods driven from floor to ceiling at their inner and outer edges. Heavy baulks of wood are slipped down between rod and door to thicken the whole. The two inner leaves are barred, ordinarily, with a timber that slips through metal hooks that latch down over it. But there are also rods to secure those, though they are seldom used. A knob at the midpoint of each rod is twisted, letting the lower rod down into its hole and sending the upper one up into its slot. If the knob is then lifted and its catch freed, it can be taken away. Then none can loosen the rods without tools and time."

"I knew that you would have all I needed to know at your tongue's tip," her husband said, laying his hand upon her hair. "We will go now, to cleanse this house of its vermin. How may we warn the lady of our coming?"

"When you are ready to make yourselves known, only cry out your name. She will know, for I have told her that you would come, if you still lived," she answered.

Without further ado, we opened the door with utmost caution and slipped into the corridor outside. The house was built sensibly with the passage that gave access to the upper rooms lying along the windowless outer wall. Thus, all the rooms were ventilated, though the hall was very dark, I am sure, even by day. The doors at our right were all firmly shut, and we tiptoed down the corridor like the shadows of ghosts.

The great stair curved downward into darkness. My light-glass, with its shielding up save for one small crack, showed us the huge doorway facing its foot. We moved downward, setting our feet near the wall and testing each step for creaks before letting our full weight upon it.

The door was massive, even for such a house as this. I held the ribbon of light while Lisaux turned the stubborn knobs, and the rods moved with muffled protest into their places. When we were sure that none might escape by this way, we turned again to the stair, walking up it in a firm and leisurely manner.

When we reached its top again, Lisaux drew his black blade. I grasped Ruif's firmly and sweat slid between my palm and the hilt, even in the chill.

My companion drew a long breath, as I did when I was about to sing. But no song came from his lips. Only a harsh and resonant, "Lisaux of the Black Shield, out of Malchion!" roared through the sleeping house.

# 9

## Dark Reckoning

THERE was a moment much like that which comes after lightning strikes nearby—a stunned silence when the world seems to hang in suspension. Then heavy feet struck the floor and doors opened onto the passageway. From someplace in the darkness came the sound of a scuffle and a blow. I felt sure that the Lady of Holdorn had seized her chance and was harrying whichever of those ruffians had molested her that night.

There was little time for imaginings, though, for several sets of booted and unbooted feet came with a rush down the corridor. Feeling that light might aid us more than it did our enemies, I unshielded my glass and set it high on a wall bracket.

It shone on three men, two barelegged with shirttails flapping, one with his breeches on but fastened all awry. They all held blades that gleamed wickedly in the light. I stood back, watchfully, and let Lisaux meet their rush. My reach was pitifully short, and my endurance was but a fraction of his in the stress of swordplay. So I guarded his back and his left side, keeping my eyes upon whichever of his foes was not immediately engaged with him.

Villains though they were, they were crafty swordsmen.

Two busied the black blade, and the third crept around the wall in shadow, hoping to take Lisaux from the side. Seeing a woman behind the black-clad warrior, the man discounted me and lunged for my friend's armpit.

I met him with steel. Unskilled as I was in the finer points of blade and footwork, I kept my tactics simple, catching him under the ribs in the midst of his lunge. A gout of blood followed my blade as I drew it forth, and he fell almost under Lisaux's feet. Sheathing my blade for a moment, I seized one unbooted foot and dragged the corpse away, that it might not trip my companion. Seeing no better way, I tumbled it down the stair, holding my eyes from following its ungainly journey from top to bottom.

Then, regaining my sword, I stepped behind Lisaux, who had been given breathing space while his opponents watched the fall of their comrade. As if realizing that they had two serious foes before them, they separated, one moving toward Lisaux, the other edging along the wall until he gained the end of the corridor. I saw the purpose of it, and I set my back to Lisaux's.

They were no cowards, those two, however ill their characters. Seeing that we were not to be tricked, they came in fast, using every bit of guile that their weapon-beset lives had taught them. It did them no good turn, for Lisaux knew all that they had ever learned, and more. And I—I was tingling from head to foot with the Power, though the song I sang was lisped with a tongue of steel.

My hand knew well, before my eyes could see, the direction of each of the man's strokes. It moved to parry them with an awful accuracy, as if a will and skill other than my own directed it. My feet took up the rhythm of the battle, and I was able to move as swiftly and effectively as did my opponent. Twice my hand all but disarmed him, sliding along his blade with my own, then giving a sudden spiraling motion that almost took the blade from his grasp.

And when the moment came, that hand thrust through his throat, felling him, gasping in his own blood, before me. I could feel that my companion had also stilled. I leaned for a moment against his back; then I retched, stumbled to the stair rail, and vomited into the darkness below.

A hand touched my shoulder. "Feel no shame, Singer. So did I, when I killed my first man, and he not so ill a bit of work as yonder two. They attacked you, thinking to fell the easy victim first. You were, I think, held up by the gods and the Mother, for I could not aid you, being beset by the best swordsman of the three."

I drew a shuddering breath and wiped my mouth on the bit of cloth I kept in my pocket for cleaning my hands before eating. When I stood upright again, there was a bit of tremor in my legs, but I soon steadied.

"We still have two to seek out," Lisaux said in a low voice. "One is with the Lady, I feel certain. The other . . . the other is either a coward, or else he is too clever entirely. We must find how those two stand."

I nodded. Then I hurried softly down the corridor to Leeana's door and whispered through it, "Which room is the chamber of Mayanna, my Lady?"

Her voice answered me, "Two doors from mine, near the end of this corridor."

I flashed my light, and Lisaux came to my side. Together we approached that door. He set his heel gently against the latch. Then he drew back and kicked out violently. The door flew open in a crash of splintered wood and twisted metal.

My lightglass showed a scene of confusion. Broken chairs and an overturned writing table lay a-scramble. The big bed was half denuded of its hangings, which draped in a twist over the bed and the floor. The Lady Mayanna stood against the right-hand wall, holding a broken lamp glass against the throat of a squat blond man whose bowels had loosened with fear, filling the room with the stench of him.

When the light gleamed in upon him, he gave a convulsive leap, pushing the woman away from him. He went through the window, taking thin curtaining and glass pane with him. Lisaux hurried to the window, while I went to the side of the woman, who was laying the broken glass aside as carefully as if it were the treasure of her life.

She turned to me blindly, and I caught her about the shoulders. She was tall, but she stooped and laid her head against my shoulder for a long moment. Then she straightened and lifted her head. I could see her gather her strength and purpose about her as if it were a disarranged robe. When Lisaux beckoned to us, she went with me to his side, and we looked out the opening into the snowlit garden.

The Beast was toying with the refugee, loping along behind him until he reached his utmost speed then drawing up beside him and tripping him into a tumble of bare legs, awkward elbows, and snow. Round and round she harried him, until he staggered. The sound of his panting breaths came clearly to us above.

When he could run no more, she swatted him flat, caught him by the scruff of his neck, and dragged him to the kitchen door. Mayanna turned and hurried toward the kitchen. We went with her, though we spared attention for shadows and nooks along the way. That fifth scoundrel was still unaccounted for.

Unbarring the heavy door, Lisaux grunted, "This one we will keep. There are questions to answer . . . and those of Holdorn have the right to deal with him as they choose, when the questioning is done. Your menfolk, Lady, will be filled with rage that must have some outlet, when they come home again."

As we dragged the man inside and secured him to one of the settles, Mayanna sank upon the other. Though her head was still high, tears were forming in her eyes. "They went, though we knew the danger that we always face here, to aid the Garloek, who were beset by wolves among their flocks. Our few laborers were deemed enough protection for the children and for me. But they were caught out upon the Plain as they tended the sheep or brought the winter's wood from the hills. They were killed, one by one, by those *ehebelothe,* and their bodies lie under the snow, unburied.

"They have been away, my men, far longer than they should have been. Weeks, not months, was the time set for their return. Yet I cannot feel that my man and our tall sons are dead. Some need has kept them overtime, and I have been unable to slip away to the pigeonloft to find if any message has come from them."

I looked at her sharply. "You of the Sunken Plain send messages by the winged ones? Can you send, then, to Garloek and to Endeor, now that you are free, asking your folk to return?"

She stood and made for the door. "I can, and I will," she called over her shoulder. "Find food and look to Leeana. I will return soon."

Lisaux hurried after her and put into her hands a great knife, such as butchers use in dismembering beasts. "There is yet another of the villains loose in or about your home, Lady. Be cautious, and carry this."

She smiled. It was a pitiful shadow of a smile, but it proved to me that she was still capable, given the chance, of reaping happiness from her life. Then she was gone, her soft footfalls inaudible three paces from the doorway. The Beast, pausing only to look into the face of her captive, followed Mayanna, and Lisaux and I sighed. She would be safe, whoever waited in the shadows of the house.

We turned our attention to breakfast. The first hint of dawn was whitening the sky beyond the garden wall. We felt the growlings of hunger in our middles, for we had made a long journey on short rations.

Thick slices of a hanging haunch were soon sizzling on the spit, as the fire of good dry wood popped away below it. A round loaf from the larder, together with a hard cheese and a pat of butter from the cold box that seemed a cupboard but was open to the chill of the outside world, through louvered venting, were soon on the round table.

While I watched the meat, Lisaux went abovestairs to see to Leeana. As I leaned over the fire, I felt the eyes of the bound man boring into my side. Ignoring him, I laid the hot meat upon a platter, replaced it with fresh slices, and set the plate to keep warm upon the hearth.

Then I turned and said to him, "What would you have, ravisher of children? Do you think it more fitting to sit at your ease there, throwing boots at the Lady in whose house you are?"

He started and looked about uneasily. I laughed. "No witchcraft, foolish man; we looked in upon you as you sat by the fire. We three had pursued you for many leagues, and Lisaux for many more than that. We rejoiced to see you at our mercy. You should be grateful to the Winter Beast. We would have killed you along with your companions, had you been with them, or from the window, if you had not been her captive."

He grunted an expletive. I have made no study of such things, and it was only noise to me. Then he whispered, "Who be ye? Clad as a man, ye be no boy. What woman goes about so?"

"Have you never heard of the Soul-Singers of Tyrnos?" I asked. I watched with interest as his dirty face paled to sallow gray. "I am of their number, though I am young and inexperienced in many facets of my craft. Still, I have been trained since childhood to sing the souls of men and of beasts . . . even plants and inanimate things. I have other skills that I am only now beginning to recognize. Have you met none of my sort in your . . . journeyings?"

He made no answer, but the sick dread on his face told me that he had no great desire to look upon the truth of his own soul.

I laughed again. "Have no fear of me, scourer of dregs. I never waste my gift or call upon the Power for any but worthy causes. Your soul is written on your face for all to see. No need of a Singing for you. Even the Beast knows you infallibly for what you are."

Then there was silence, while the meat popped and sizzled, spattering hot missiles of grease into the fire. I listened past the homely noises, hoping to hear some movement or breath that might indicate to me the place where the last of Ruif's men was hiding. There was nothing to hear except the beginning spat of new snow against the window, the dim mutter of voices from abovestairs, and the rough breathing of our prisoner. Time seemed, for a little, to slow to a crawl. In my weary state, I began to wonder if this entire situation might not be some fevered dream from which I would soon awaken.

The click of the Beast's toenails roused me from my lethargy. I looked up to see her enter the room, followed by a much-altered Mayanna. She had washed herself, wound her red-gold hair high, and secured it with a black comb. She had changed her drab robe for one of sea-green, whose simple cut emphasized the supple elegance of her tall body. A queen might have looked less worthy of reverence, however richly dressed.

Her recent trials and indignities had worn her pale golden face into gaunt contours, had deepened, I was sure, the lines on her brow and about her eyes. But her dignity and her courage shone forth from her eyes unabated. The Holdorn must be a man to admire, if he deserved the wife he had chosen.

86

The man on the bench paled when he saw her. He twisted his bound wrists as if to loose them. His feet made running motions, though they were secured to the base of the settle.

Mayanna looked down upon him. "Garz," she said, and the name was a curse that might not have been improved upon. "I will lay no hand upon you, who aided in the violation and death of my children, who laid your hands upon me in cruelty and lust. That is the prerogative of Hanrik, the Holdorn. I have laid blows on your putrid flesh, slashed your skin with broken glass. That is my share of vengeance. He will have none, perhaps, to wreak vengeance on save only you. I will not stay him, whatever he chooses to do."

If it were possible, Garz would have gone even more pale. As it was, he rivaled the snow that tapped against the window. Even the fire at his elbow failed to warm his face with its ruddy glow. He slumped against the back of the settle as if his spine had gone to jelly. Mayanna laughed and turned from him to go about her work.

When Lisaux and Leeana came down the stairway, breakfast steamed on the table. Mayanna had drawn up a vessel from a hidden well in the scullery and taken from it a jug of fresh goat's milk. We sat at a laden table and ate as if we had forgotten the taste of food.

Garz refused to eat.

The Beast had indicated that she wished to go out into the Plain, but when we had finished our meal she was back at the kitchen door, her short tail tucked around her toes, licking her whiskers and grinning through the driven snow-flakes. Upon entering the house, she glanced about the room, nodded to see Mayanna clearing away the dishes. Then she looked into my eyes, and I felt yet again the force of her willing that I understood.

"She wants us to go back upstairs to the room where Ruif lies," I said to Lisaux. "I cannot tell why, but she feels that this must be done immediately."

He nodded, and we hurried away after the Beast, who fled along the dark passage as if she were a shadow herself. The door to the chamber was open when we drew near, and the Beast leaped inside without giving any warning of her approach.

There was a gasp of surprise. We stepped into the doorway in time to see yet another of the men we had pursued leap through a closed window out into the snowy garden. Lisaux peered into the snow, seeking that fleeing figure, as the Beast caught my hand in her mouth and drew me toward the bed where the grisly remains of Ruif lay amid the blood.

At first, I saw nothing that had not been there before. Then, at the opening between the neck buttons of the fouled shirt, I caught the gleam of gold. With much distaste, I caught the chain and drew from its hiding place a velvet pouch that swung from the fine-linked gold. As I held it, my hand told me something that my head refused, for a moment, to accept.

"Lisaux!" I breathed. He turned from the window and came to my side.

"What is it, Singer? You are paler than Garz, and your hand is shaking."

"Open me this packet, my Friend," I quavered. "If what I believe is within it, then my world has turned awry, and all that I believed true must be false."

He clumsily drew out the strings that my shaking hands could not manage. Into his left hand fell a gleaming medallion that sparkled with pale blue gems outlining the *Huym*. My breath left me in a rush, and the world swam before my eyes.

Lisaux's rough grasp at my elbow brought me to myself. "What is this thing? And why does it terrify you, who have shown no fear in the face of terrors that would have shaken a seasoned warrior?"

88

For answer, I pulled up the sleeve of my leather garment and lifted my arm, so he could see the symbol branded into the curve of my elbow. "That is the sign of Singers. *Huym,* the symbol of music and truth. And Tyrnos is undone, Lisaux of the Black Shield!"

# 10

## *The Counselings of Wrath*

WE had no fear that our quiet lurker might escape across the Plain in the teeth of the blizzard that was now blowing. He must take shelter or die. We went down to ask Mayanna what his prospects might be of finding a place to escape the rigor of the weather.

"He will lie quiet in the shepherd's hut to southward," she answered. "He must know it, for he and his friends searched the lands all about, seeking out all our people who might give aid to me. The hut is cared for only by a woman, and it is stocked well with fuel and dried mutton and fruit. Until the storm lifts, you may be certain that he is there."

"Then we, too, may lie quiet and rest," said Lisaux. "But when that villain moves, we will be upon his trace, eh, Singer?" He looked at me with his dark eyes sparkling.

I thought for a long moment. So compelling had been each step in my journeying that I had felt little volition in the matters I pursued. Now there was time to rest, to take stock, to determine where my duties lay. I looked at Leeana and Mayanna, and something turned hard and stubborn in my heart. Be it right or wrong, I must follow this way.

"If you wish to make one with my cause, friend, I will be happy. It may be that the pursuit of this one brigand will lead to nothing. It may be that it will guide us into the paths I must take to undertake the reformation of my country. If even one Singer is tainted with the darkness of him who gave the *Huym* to Ruif, then there is sore ill here. It is in my mind that a rot has touched the very root of my order, there in the Citadel, which is the heart of Tyrnos.

"Those who hunger after Power lay their hands upon the powerful. So I was taught, and, truly, if the High King and his advisers are lost to virtue, they must have tainted her who is Soul-Singer to the King. She would paint his iniquity upon the walls of the city, otherwise. We on the edges of the land might well slip from mind. Busy about our work in the remote parts of Tyrnos, we would seem to be no threat, I should think. Those who were part of the Citadel, though, would be in peril . . . unless, indeed, they might be at the source of the problem."

I turned to Lisaux and whispered, "The Ethran in whose house you hung for so long said that he was not alone upon our world. It may be that one of the gray ones dwells now in the house of the High King."

We looked at one another in grim speculation until Leeana put her hand on my wrist.

"Let it not weigh upon your heart, Singer. You have accomplished things that none would have thought possible for one so young and so small. Singer or no, you have a strong heart and an agile mind. If you and my husband decide upon the fates of the great ones of Tyrnos, it will surprise me little if that comes to pass. Now sit before the fire and rest. Or go up to one of the many rooms above and sleep, for you will need all possible endurance in time to come."

I dropped into a low chair beside the table, fully in the firelight, and the Beast came and curled at my feet, yawning. My eyes grew heavy as her head settled onto the arch of my foot, and we dozed together as Leeana, Lisaux, and Mayanna talked in low voices.

Elysias's voice moved through my dream. "It is in my mind that you may be the Chosen of this generation . . ." The words echoed in my heart. For the first time I comprehended that this strange quest I had entered upon might truly be the great work of my generation.

Half waking, half sleeping, I considered the question. The gods, she had told me, never choose unworthy instruments. And the gods, I could not doubt, had made me to be as I was, a questioner of traditions, a breaker of rules, an innovator in a calling that taught acceptance and conformity. Those traits had made me choose as I had done, since the moment Razul rode me down. Each decision had set me deeper into a powerful tide of events. At any point, if I had made the decisions my training called for, I would have been steered away from this tide of circumstance into trivial eddies . . . or death.

In that midpoint of clarity that stands between waking and sleep, I saw the Ethran, not as a temporary threat to my own safety, but as part of a peril that might well affect my entire world. The path of Lisaux, that of the Beast, and my own had been drawn together into a firm twist, like cordage. It would not, I half dreamed, end here. We were caught up in a giant weaving . . . weaving . . . weaving . . .

I woke to the bustle of preparation that spoke of another meal. The two women refused my aid, pushing me back into the comfort of my chair. I sat there watching the bright picture they made, one so tall and stately, all red-gold and green, the other slender as her husband's blade, silver-blonde, and gray of dress. Without strong coloring, but holding the eye with her shining aura.

A thought occurred to me, and I asked, "How long will it take, Lady of Holdorn, for your birds to reach their goals?"

"They are there, by now," she answered. "They travel in hours the leagues that men require days to cover."

"Then how many days might it take your men to come from Garloek, if they are still there?"

"In fair weather, three days will see the journey done. In this storm, in ordinary times, five or six would be required. But I sent with the pigeons the message, 'Return at once,' together with that of 'Death and dishonor.' They will come as if the gods empowered their limbs and their hearts. They will leave horses lame behind them and come forward afoot, if need be. They will be here when dawn breaks in two days' time."

I nodded. "As I thought . . . and hoped. Do you think, Mayanna, that your folk will give ear to my surmisings? Will they join with me in the cleansing of Tyrnos, if that must be done?"

Her gray eyes flashed. "They would do the task alone, Singer, if they knew the way. With you and the Beast and the gods, not to say the Black Shield, they will walk into the Citadel and hold blade to the High King's throat. We are of one mind, Hanrik and I, in most things of this world, and I have no doubt of his decision in this."

Reassured, I ate the noon meal in drowsy abstraction. Then, lulled by the spat of snow, I sought a chamber at the other end of the house from that in which Ruif's body lay and fell headlong into sleep, the Beast warm against my side.

Those whom the gods use strongly are left empty, for a time after. The endurance that had borne me up for so long gave way to the demands of the flesh. I slept through two nights and a day, to be waked by the hallooing of deep voices, the clashing of arms onto the stone floor of the kitchen, and the voice of Mayanna rising above the hubbub.

I rose then and washed myself. Someone had kept a small blaze burning on the hearth of my chamber, and my leather garments were laid over a stool before it. They had been oiled and rubbed, and they were warm and supple as I pulled on the jerkin and breeches.

Once clad, I stretched my arms wide and rose to my toes, feeling out my body. Then I smiled with satisfaction. I was myself again, though I was hungry enough to chew boots.

Emerging from my chamber, I went softly down the corridor to the door behind which Ruif had lain. The door opened to a touch, and I saw that the room had been cleaned, its gory tenant removed, and the window replaced. I looked long at the bed, to which hangings had been restored. Its brown homespun coverlet was fresh, as were the lacy pillows at its head. Mayanna's hands had been busy at removing all trace of her late guest.

I would have given much to ask whatever spirit still haunted the place one question: Who among the hierarchy of Singers had last owned that jewelled symbol he had worn about his neck? But the voices of the dead are chancy and difficult to rouse. I dared not risk singing the dead, simply to make my own task easier. If that procedure proved fatal to me, who would then be able to direct the wrath of my companions?

I turned on my heel and went down to the kitchen, from which a babble of talk was issuing. I could hear Leeana's light voice plainly above the rumble of male tones, but Mayanna's I could not detect.

When I entered the kitchen, I understood why. She was engulfed, tall as she was, in the all-enveloping embrace of a dark-haired man who was so large that even that big room seemed filled with his presence. Her head was against his chest, and his square hand was smoothing her hair, gently and rhythmically, as one would soothe a distressed child.

Upon his face was such wrath as I had never seen before. Though I must admit that I had looked into no mirror after the slaying of the Kalirs.

I entered the kitchen and immediately felt dwarfed. Not only was Hanrik of Holdorn a giant of a man, his sons were as tall as he, though the years had not yet girded them with the formidable bulk of muscle that their father carried. I felt as though I moved in a forest of great mang trees that were gifted with the power to speak and to walk. Never before had I felt so keenly what life must be like to a mouse.

They were, for all their size, a mannerly group of men. The first to see me came forward and bent to take my hand, then led me to Hanrik.

"This can be no other than the Singer of Souls," he said, and so noticing was his eye that he immediately sat on a nearby chair, removing his towering presence from the air above me.

I gave my hand to Hanrik, who took it in his left, his right being still occupied with his wife.

"I had wondered if the lord of Holdorn could possibly be worthy of the Lady Mayanna," I said. "I wonder no more. She needs all your tenderness, sir, for she has suffered much."

His dark blue eyes were filled with tears, as he looked down at me. "Singer, I will not only comfort her. I will follow you even into the Dark Land itself in pursuing those who caused this thing to happen."

"Then hold her on your knee, while I help Leeana to put food on the table. Are your horses tended, or should I see to them, also?"

He laughed, a great bark. "We left them to follow as they could. Their bellies will lead them home to their stalls and their grainbags. It will be morning, I'd judge, before they come. We wore them to exhaustion. Then we walked like madmen through the blizzard, linked to one another with rope, that none might stray and be lost. We could eat those selfsame horses, given the chance."

I hurried to aid Leeana, and soon we sat about that capacious board, and for a long time the Holdorn men and I ate with full attention. The others, having eaten beforehand, took up the tale of Ruif and his henchmen; and by the time we were done, the newcomers knew as much of the affair as did we.

It was well for Garz that he sat bound and helpless. Had he

been free and armed, his life would have ended with the ending of our tale. The Holdorn were gently taught, however, and they could not harm the helpless, however terrible his deeds. As it was, the four giant men rose and stood about the settle, looking down at the sweating wretch. Then they turned and said, "We must rest now, but save his questioning for us; we ask it as a courtesy."

We nodded, and they went away up the stairs, Mayanna still half hidden in her husband's cloaked arm. Then we sat, Lisaux, Leeana, the Beast, and I, about the fire. After a time, Lisaux hauled the limp Garz off to a maid's chamber nearby and settled him for the night.

When he returned, I drew the *Huym* from my tunic and held it up in the firelight. It dangled, swinging slightly, and its blue stones winked like knowing eyes. The graceful symbol they outlined had lost for me much of its reverent joy. It seemed, somehow, baleful.

We sat late, without words, thinking, I surmised, of much the same things. Then we rose to retire for the night, and I turned to Leeana, saying, "You have suffered much and lived in dread for months, Lady. This is a thing of Tyrnos. You who are of Malchion owe this unhappy land nothing save curses. If it should be that you take counsel together and decide that a return to your mountains is wisest for you, I will understand. We will go into dire circumstance, I have no doubt. Your husband will be imperiled."

She took my hand. We were almost of a height, and she looked into my eyes. "We have taken counsel, Singer, for the days and nights that you slept. Weak as I am, I am strong in anger. Lisaux is consumed with wrath. In the presence of dark wickedness, no man can say, 'I am not of the country that spawned this, so I am excused from correcting it.' All men inhabit the country of the mind and the flesh. All are harmed by ill deeds; all are smirched by the dishonor of our fellows. We can only cleanse ourselves by laying our hands to the task of making clean what part of our world we can.

"Lisaux is a warrior. He has, as well, a subtle and original mind. He will go questing with you, and you will be glad of him. I am not strong enough in body to travel in the way you will go, but I can rally those who live in the Plain, and if it is possible, I will come with all I can raise to the Citadel, after you. Mayanna and I will go forth among the families and rouse them to vigilance and to action.

"Only remember, Singer, that we value you, not simply for your gifts from the gods, but for the fact that you are a woman of courage and honor. The gods do not choose weaklings or fools for their instruments, as men do not choose flawed steel for swords or wind-broken horses for steeds. You are much, in and of yourself. We love you."

I took her hands in both of mine and kissed her forehead. Then I hurried away up the stair. Even though I had slept for so long, I fell again into dream as soon as my head touched the pillow.

Excruciatingly bright light woke me. I lay under my fur coverings and looked toward the window, where frost flowers formed lacy forests on the glass. Beyond those mysterious silver deeps, the sun was shining. After a moment, I slipped from the bed and hurried into my garments, dropping tinderwood among the coals of my fire and building it up with peat. The great logs in the shed were reserved for the cook fires belowstairs; the rooms above made do with the more plentiful peat, though it was difficult to start a-burning and made a slow fire.

When the blaze was doing well, I went to the window. The garden was a dazzle of sunlight over snow, fit to blind me, and I squinted my eyes to see what danced amid the drifts. It was, of course, the Beast. I tapped on the glass until she heard and came to stand below. Then I smiled down at her and gestured outward, over the shining Plain that I could see beyond the wall from my high window.

She opened her mouth in a fanged grin and thumped her short tail in arcs on the snow as she sat on a flawless cushion of white.

I washed myself and screened the fire. Then I hurried down the stair to find why none had waked me. All were still sleeping, exhausted with grief and exertion and anger.

I built up the fire, whose banked coals still radiated warmth, and set a cauldron of porridge to simmer at its edge. Not since I left the house of Kalir had I felt so housewifely; I almost felt Doni at my elbow, gently suggesting the best ways to slice meat without taking off fingers with the slabs. The bread cupboard was all but bare, and I ventured, greatly daring, to try making bread as she had taught me. When six long loaves were rising in the stone oven let into the side of the fireplace, I sighed with satisfaction and sat on a settle to wait for the first awakened to descend the stair.

A groan from the maid's chamber brought me up again. Garz, I had no doubt, was pretending illness in order to soften his questioning.

When I stood over him, however, I was surprised at the look of him. His skin was greenish, and he was drawn over onto his side, as if his gut were paining him. I touched his forehead. It was slick with sweat, even in the crisp chill of the room. Knowing that beasts have senses that men lack, I went to the door of the kitchen and called to my furred friend, who came lolloping through the powdery snow like a kitten at play.

She looked at me questioningly. I pointed toward the inner room. In one smooth ripple, she was beside the couch, sniffing at the man from hair to heel. When she was done, she sat back on her haunches with a little growl, as if something angered and troubled her. Her eyes again fastened onto me, and I opened my mind, trying for understanding.

One thought came to me—death. Death both imminent and painful. Without waiting to make an examination of my own,

I fled upstairs and pounded on Lisaux's door.

"Come down, Lisaux, Leeana. Garz is dying, I have no doubt. If he is to answer us at all, it must be now!" I cried. Then I turned to wake the Holdorn. When all were a-bustle, I went down again to stand beside Garz.

I washed his face with a cool cloth, tried to get a bit of herb tea down his throat; but he could not swallow. I feared that he could not even articulate, so quickly was he losing control of his muscles. The others, arriving in haste, saw the predicament without words. We stood about in anxiety and frustration, watching our only source of information approach the gates of death.

A thought came to me. "I will call upon the Power," I said aloud. "I have done so before, in things that required no singing of souls. Each time I have been offered a clue."

Lisaux, after a brief glance at Garz, nodded, as did the Holdorn. "There is no way that we can reach him now," rumbled Hanrik. "He is tortured in his own flesh beyond anything that we could have brought ourselves to do. Find what you can, Singer. We will let our vengeance go."

So I stood and closed my eyes. I breathed deeply, and the Power began to move in my veins and along my nerves. I could almost hear the deep thrumming of its presence. A harp-string must feel so, in the moment of sounding its music.

A cloud rolled over my spirit. The clarity that usually comes with the Power was subtly obscured. Dark blue-gray mists seemed to surround me. I brought from my memory the pure light of the morning outside, and reluctantly the mists rolled back a bit, leaving a space about me and the man on the bed.

From his tortured figure a dank miasma seemed to rise . . . but no! The stuff was sinking into him from above! Now I could see the individual fingers of mist creeping downward into his writhing flesh, prying at the stubborn life that persisted there. That crawling abomination shook me with revulsion. Then the Power shook me still more, and I felt as if I were filled with an energy so strong that my flesh could not contain it.

It came forth in one sustained minor note that rose, after a few heartbeats, a half-step into a clear and triumphant major tone. The sound coming from my own throat was so piercing that it pained my ears. My companions must have suffered even more.

As the note swelled through the chill air, a change took place in the mist. It turned bluish and began to pale, its motion slowing to a stop. Then, in wavering lines that became a coherent pattern, the *Huym* scrawled itself across the face of the mist.

There was a moment of silence. Another note strained at me, and I uttered a sound so high, so clear, so bell-like that I marveled that it had come from my body.

The *Huym* shattered away to nothing. The mist winked out as if it had never been.

I sank onto the floor, spine straight, to sit. My legs were no longer capable of holding me.

# 11

## A Grim Adventuring

THE Holdorn, nearest to me, stooped and lifted me again to my feet, sustaining me there by the aid of his arm. Together we looked upon Garz.

The greenish pallor had changed. Now his face was gray with the approach of death, but his pain seemed to have eased. No trace of the mist was left about him. The sickish odor that had been in the room was gone, and a tingling freshness had taken its place. As we looked, the man's eyes opened.

For the first time, the human being that Garz had been looked out of his eyes. He had been a villain, there was no doubt of it. Theft and rapine had been his life. I could read it on him as if it were traced in symbols upon his skin. But the flesh-crawling wickedness that he had emitted was gone from him.

Still aided by the Holdorn, I moved nearer the bedside. Bending, I asked softly, "Have you a blue-gemmed symbol, Garz, as did Ruif?"

His throat worked, but no sound came forth. His head moved on the pillow in a slight nod, and he fumbled in his tunic and drew out a small medallion. Not golden, not flashing with those glowing jewels, but still traced with the *Huym* in bits of blue stone. When I took it from his hand, he sighed as if some burden had been lifted from him.

"Who gave this to you—or to Ruif to give to you?" I asked.

"One came from the south," he croaked. "We sat in the Eruifal keep in the mountains of Malchion. We had nothing but wantings and rememberings among us all. Ruif was dour, staring away across the peaks toward the place where Leeana lived. We were left to gamble for stones and quarrel among ourselves."

He gasped and almost choked. Mayanna brought watered wine, which Lisaux coaxed down him. It brought a lessening of the grayness, a strengthening of his voice as he resumed his tale. "When winter wore to spring, a rider came from the south and shut himself into Ruif's chamber. He was an unchancy being, one I'd not have trusted even so much as one of us. When he came forth again, his face gray and his robe gray and his eyes hidden under his wide hat brim, we all shuddered and made luck signs. But he rode away again without staying for food or for rest." He choked, and Lisaux gave him more wine.

"Then Ruif came from his chamber, and he was a man changed past recognition. 'We have been given a thing of power,' he told us. 'All that we desire will be ours, the old adventurings, the old plunderings, the old games with maidens and with boys will begin again, and none may stay us from them!'

"Then he gave to each of us a medal like this; and from the moment it hung about my neck, I felt myself to be someone I did not know and could not fathom. Much that we did in the wild months just past is lost in fog to my memory." He paused for a long time, his breathing growing rough again.

"Am I the last?" he asked suddenly.

He looked at me, and I nodded and said, "You are the last but one left alive of the six who came to Holdorn."

He sighed a great breath. "We were cursed, you know," he said. "Something compelled us along the old path we knew before . . . but we were never quite so callous before Ruif gave us the symbols. Something moved through us . . ." and that was the last word of all.

We looked at one another, wordlessly. Then Lisaux pulled the covering over the staring face, and we went into the kitchen.

"He was hale and well last night," the Black Shield murmured. "Something moved across the lands to slay him."

"Or this called something to him for that purpose," I said, holding the medallion so that the dull blue eyes caught the light from the windows and winked balefully.

"Build up the fire, if you will, my friends, so I may bake my bread . . . and destroy this wicked thing." I laid the thing in the coals and watched the heat run over it in quivers and the stones melt and ooze away like tears. Then I set the bread in the baking ovens and opened the dampers that fed heat into them. The *Huym* I banished to the back of my mind. But a cold sickness was in me, for now I knew that the Ethrans were working in all of Tyrnos.

While the bread baked, the men once again removed a corpse from Holdorn Keep, stowing it under a cairn of stones until spring would allow burial. When they were finished with their grim task, cleaned from their labors, and ravenous, the breakfast I had made was ready. My spirit was leaden, however, and I had no appetite.

The Beast watched us eat, then begged her freedom and ran away into the bright day. While she was gone, I set my fellows down in the settles and chairs and said, "I dare not waste this weather. When I sang for snow, I little knew how much the gods would send. It may be storming again by night, but in a day's time I can go far on my road southward. Lisaux has agreed to go with me. It seems to my mind that, for what we must do, that is enough. How think you of Holdorn?"

Hanrik looked about at his tall sons, meeting their eyes, one by one, and as he did so each nodded. "We Holdorn are with you; but there are others upon the Plain who have suffered strange troubles. They are angry and disturbed, and we believe that they will make common cause with us, if they are led. We propose to lead them."

I looked doubtful, but Hanrik said, "See it thus, Singer: If we can raise an army from the Plain, we can follow you. You will know that a force of arms comes at your heels, though no one else in the Citadel would believe it. No sane general begins a campaign in winter.

"You are but two, and you can slip into the walls in any of a thousand ways, without suspicion being aroused. What you learn there, what you can accomplish by means of the Power that the gods have given you, I cannot know. Yet it is better to have an army and never need it than to need one and be without."

Lisaux nodded, a short jerk of his head. "He speaks truly, Singer. None will suspect two winter-nipped travelers. We can go where we will and find what we can. Then, in a few days, the Holdorn can perhaps have an array of armed men on the road to the Citadel. If the snows continue as they have been, no word will find its way to the High King until it is too late. We do not know, any more than does the Holdorn, what we will find or what will be needed to correct it."

So it was agreed; Lisaux and I made ready our packs and bade our friends farewell, though the parting with Leeana was painful for my companion. We set forth well before noon, the Beast capering about us in the snow as if she were setting forth upon a frolic. It had also been agreed upon that she, unable to enter the city with us, would be the liaison with our rear guard. For that purpose she wore a collar of white fur, fitted with a pouch beneath her chin in which messages could be placed. Leeana and the Lady of Holdorn had rifled old trunks until they found fur that matched her own coat. Then they had taken pains that it might fit so unobtrusively that none might know it for what it was.

The day was so brilliant that we muffled our heavy hoods about our faces, leaving only a slit for seeing. Otherwise, the light might well have blinded us. The sun, glaring over all the expanse of snow, seemed without heat; only light poured from the white disk that stared from mid-heaven.

The cold was devastating. Fur-lined boots from Holdorn enveloped my own russet ones, with fuzzy woollen socks inside. Still my toes went numb and my blood seemed charged with ice as it moved through the veins in my feet. Fur tunic, fur leggings, fur cloak from Rellas's house did their best, but inside them all, I was cold.

There was only one way to move through such weather . . . fast and without stopping. Had we been still in the mang forest, we might have fared better, but here there was no shelter from the thin breeze that sliced out of the north, trying, it seemed, to sever our breath from our bodies. I was almost tempted to sing again, calling for less demanding weather. On consideration, however, I realized that it was our ally, if we could but survive it.

Lisaux moved ahead, his longer legs breaking a path for me through the crust. I set my eyes on his pack, so tall that his head was hidden behind it, and trudged along. One foot—right! One foot—left! The protesting leg muscles, unused to the strange footing of the frozen snow, cramped and eased and cramped again. I ignored them. The overbearing will that our training provides moved my body along as if a puppet master swung me along on strings to his command.

So the sun moved overhead and downward. The Beast, giving over her play, came sedately behind me, sheltering my back from the wind with her furry presence. The clear air made distances deceptive, and the spur of rock toward which we moved seemed to back away from us as we traveled. Now it loomed so near in the lucid day that I could count individual boulders upon its base. Now it retreated into the distance until I could barely make out its shape.

We had hoped to come to that spot before nightfall, but we soon realized that darkness would find us still unsheltered in the midst of the snow. We ate while walking, munching fresh bread and dried fruits and thin-sliced meat, but we were so fogged with weariness that all might have been sawdust. The Beast, coming watchfully behind us, deigned to accept meat, instead of hunting abroad as she usually did. And when the time came that my will was unable to make my body move in a steady and purposeful line, she nudged me with her nose. Then she moved past me to nudge Lisaux.

He was, I suspected, moving in as tranced a state as I, and he started when she touched him. Without waiting for him to respond, she moved aside from our path until she found a great drift that must have covered some obstruction. This she dug into with energy, making the snow fly out behind her in great white wings.

When the snow ceased flying, she disappeared into the hole she had made for a moment. Then she came out and urged us into it. We found that she had trampled out a space like a bubble under the snow, large enough for all three to crouch or to lie. We fumbled in our packs and drew out the big fur blankets that added so much weight to our burdens. When they were arranged under and over us, with the Beast snugly between, we found, surprisingly, that we were more comfortable than we had been since leaving Holdorn.

The thin drift of air that came through the small opening she had left when she blocked the entry hole was just enough to keep us from feeling stifled. We plunged into sleep as divers plummet into deep waters.

Only to dream . . .

I moved through thin veils of mist. The cold was only a memory, for the mist was warm as steam from soup. Walls thrust through the grayness. They were of stone, but they seemed oddly tenuous. I had the feeling that the mist was wafting in and out through them. There was light, though it, too, was grayish.

Still, it was not the death-gray of the Ethran. It was a living gray like the bark of a brook-tree or the morning breath that hangs over water in first light. There were silvery glints reflected from the walls, as if tiny lightnings played through the steamy air about me. My eyes were befooled by the play of glint and shadow, and I looked hard at the wall for a gate or a door whereby I might enter.

I was alone. Though I looked back, seeking for some sign of those who had been my companions, there was no shape, no footfall to reassure me. I turned and pressed my hands against the stone, feeling along it for an opening. Six paces sidewise took me to such a spot, where a wooden door was let into the thickness of the wall. It was old, old, and the weather had so worn away the grain of the wood that it felt to my fingers as if it were grooved.

Startled, I looked down for the fur mittens that I had worn, but my hands were bare. I was clad in a loose robe of gray stuff so filmy that it did not hang from my shoulders but floated restlessly about me. My feet, too, were bare, but the spongy turf beneath them was so warm that they made no protest.

Accepting this, as one does in a dream, I pressed my hands flat against the door. It resisted for a moment; then it moved grudgingly inward, grating on gravels just inside. I nudged it far enough to admit my sidling form and slipped through the crack into a garden as gray as the outside had been.

Across the space, beyond a fountain that played silver-gray light into gray-silver air, was an open door that poured a flood of white light across the gray velvet of the sward. It sliced like a blade through the indecisive illumination of the place, and I moved toward it without caution or hesitation.

As I went, I felt about me whisperings of motion. From the

corners of my eyes, I almost saw figures darker than the misty air. Still, there was no hint or feel of menace. I felt that curiosity brought those shadows about me, and I moved through them freely.

I stepped through that arched door into a hall filled with brightness. Its capacious size was as full of light as an overflowing cup is full of water. It was curved to right and to left in a strange manner. Or so it seemed to me, used to straight lines and square angles that marked off space into stringent geometries.

A blaze burned on the hearth at the back of the hall. Before it, huddled close despite the steamy heat, were three chairs, their backs toward me. From the spot where I stood, I could see one pale right hand stretched along a heavy chair arm, one elbow clad in shimmery gray stuff, and one spidery-thin left hand that tapped its fingers on the arm of the last chair.

I cleared my throat, suddenly shy, for all my training. There was neither movement nor a turning to see who entered the hall. Then I took myself in hand and walked forward over the rush-strewn flags of the floor.

"The gods give you grace," I said clearly. "I am come to the summoning of dream, which leads me to your door."

There was a moment of stillness. Then the hands and the elbow vanished, to be replaced by three tall figures that stood, turning slowly, and regarded me gravely with eyes unlike those of any living being I had ever met. They were gray eyes, yet they were as bright and changeful as swift brooks in the mountains. They were old and young and wise and full of merriment and sadness.

They were tall women, thin amid their floating gray robes, with silver hair that was coiled high and stabbed with silver pins that caught the light and reflected it. They seemed as tenuous as the mists in their garden, but I felt a terrible strength in them. It was strength alien to those the gods lent to me, yet it was in some way kindred. Their eyes held all that

I had been taught to value, and they were free of fear and its attendant cruelty.

The one on the left, she of the long right hand, said, "You have come, first of the three, to our summoning. We find in you a measure of potency that is not usual in your kind. You are not of the alien breed, we are sure, yet you are unlike your fellows that we have known through the ages. Name yourself."

Strangely, I did not hesitate. "My mother called me Yeleeve," I replied, "but I left that name behind, when I became a Singer of Souls. We who sing the souls of men answer to no name. We are possessed of nothing, not even so slight a thing as that. I have the flesh in which I stand and the voice that tenants it. I count myself rich beyond desiring."

There was a ripple of breath, as if they sighed in unison. "So . . ." the second said, she of the elbow. "The ones who guard the fates of men have not forsaken them, in all the long years of striving and frustration. Perhaps, Sisters . . ." she looked to right and to left ". . . we lost heart too soon . . ."

But there was no reply.

Then the last bent upon me a gaze as chill as the wind in the Plain where my body still slept. She looked me up and down and through and through. I felt that she knew both my past and my future; that I had been winnowed of every vestige of substance there was in me. Then she spoke. "You are not afraid, Child of Men. You undertake a terrible task, knowing its perils. You are full of concern for the well-being of your fellows."

There was no taint of sarcasm in her words, but I suddenly found my confidence shaken. Was I simply a youngling, inexperienced, anxious to teach my teachers? Was I, in very fact, savoring the taste of power over my fellows that I had been given?

I shuddered, my bare feet feeling suddenly cold. I moved toward and between the women to kneel before their fire. It gave no heat, only light, whiter than the sun on snow. It penetrated my flesh and my mind and my heart, as I knelt there. I gave myself up to it.

The women moved behind me, but I could not turn to see what they did. I was enveloped in cool flame, and the world was lost in the mists.

# 12

## All Colors Are in Gray

IT is a strange thing to see the world from an alien dimension. The ordinary facets of living, the mere angles and planes of the things we take for granted, are suddenly warped askew. One sees them as if for the first time. So it was when I entered into the fire of the Gray Sisters.

It seemed as if every atom of my being was individually washed in that whiteness. The tensions and interactions that hold the flesh into unity seemed loosed and dissolved. I spread onto the air like mist, while that brilliancy forced me outward from myself. When I was laid like a chance breeze across the air of the chamber, the three women looked upward.

"Thus you can learn truth, small sister. Your form impresses its own demands and prejudices upon the spirit within, shaping its judgments into a limited set of molds. Now go free, for a time. Look into the world that is yours; look into us; look, most of all, into yourself. When you have done, we will see . . ."

A gust of wind took me with it, out through the not-quite-walls. I spiraled high, looking down onto the strange blur that was the place where those gray women dwelled. All about it were the fields of snow that covered all the Plain except that spot. Towering just to south of it was the spur of rock that had led us through the day. I went up, borne by the strangely self-contained wind. Soon I could see the great scarp to the east, down which we had come. It loomed as a dark line across the snow-lit night, and the forest that sparsely lined its edge grew thicker, the more to eastward I could see.

To the west, the Plain lay, seeming unbroken in the flat glimmer of the snow. The hills that edged it were too far for seeing at night, even with the superlative vision that had been lent to me for this venture. To northward, I could see a tiny glow that marked the windows of Holdorn. I felt a tug of affection that almost diverted me from the direction in which the wind seemed determined to take me.

I resisted that tug, and the triumphant wind bore me higher and higher until the whole of the Plain, the entire forest through which we had traveled, the very lands about Razul and the house of Rellas lay beneath me. Even the mountains of Malchion loomed dimly on the edge of the northern sky, dark against the teeming stars.

I hung in a sky that seemed frozen into stillness. So clear was the air that I seemed almost to hang among the stars themselves, as I looked down at my country. Then I became aware of something strange.

I could feel, as if against the skin I no longer possessed, every life that breathed below me: every life that grew in the steady, slow manner of tree and plant; every life that hopped or burrowed or swam. Most strangely of all, I could feel the lives of men and women. They were like small fires, banked against the night. From each came a warmth, a faint glow, that was apparent to my altered senses.

I could focus my attention upon one, and it would seem to expand until I stood within the self that held the life. If it waked, I saw through its eyes and moved among its thoughts. If it slept, I knew its dreams. When I moved from it, I knew that soul as though it were my own. Not one of the spirits I learned seemed aware of my presence.

I moved from one to another, drawn, seemingly, to those most involved in the life of Tyrnos. I saw through the eyes of a wakeful drover, newly returned from the south and sleepless with worry over the strangeness he found there. I walked through the dreams of a lord greater than Razul. He, too, was troubled. In his dreams he questioned the High King's Minister, though the questions his sleeping mind formulated were a hodgepodge of sense and nonsense.

Only a short span was required for my forays, and by the time the night wind took me, once again, in its grip. I must have studied a hundred of my fellows. I had no time to muse over what I had learned, for the wind bore me outward. No closer approximation can I give than that, for I could detect neither upward nor downward motion, nor any to either side. Still, I was elsewhere, and in that dimension I saw the ladies of the mist drawing nearer and nearer to me.

I knew them to be the same; but in no manner did they resemble women of my race. They hung as columns of mist that swirled gently in circles about the central cores. Every color played within their beings, making dim rainbows in the eery light that illuminated the dimension into which I had been taken. Though they were still, save for that swirling, they were intensely busy. I could feel that with every augmented sense I possessed.

I almost felt as if the wind were also a thinking spirit, for it chuckled as it bore me into the midst of those gray pillars. Then it set me to cycling gently, in time with the Sisters. Like thread from a spindle, knowledge spun into me. The proud and confident self I had always been dwindled to a mere fleck, while I marveled at the beings among whom I found myself.

For they, too, were gods, those Gray Sisters. Not aliens, as the Ethran had been; not human as Lisaux and I were; not a thinking kind as was the Beast, though clothed in different flesh. They were of the family of the gods.

It is one of the Mysteries kept close within the Singers and those of the Order of Healers: The gods are not invisible, untouchable, unfathomable divinities. They are beings subject to Law, as we are; though they are not made of the stuff of worlds, they are obedient to laws that are inscrutable to our limited vision. They are not limited to one time and one place, as we are. They move freely between what was and what will be. They care for the morsels of flesh that they find grubbing about on the worlds within their scope.

It may seem strange that this is kept as a Mystery. Some have thought that we should share such reassuring knowledge with our fellows. So I thought, before I left the security of the School. It took only a very short time for me to learn that common folk want no easily understood gods. They desire incomprehensible and capricious tyrants for their objects of worship. Some comfort seems to come to them with the belief that they are the helpless victims of uncontrollable Fates.

Yet I whirled among gods, and from them came a constant aura of concern. What their work might have been, I cannot know. Perhaps they managed the tides and the winds. Maybe they oversaw the sprouting of seeds and the opening of buds —or the fall of snow. However it may have been, I knew without doubt that they were busy about the caretaking of the physical world I knew.

I thought of the thing one had said—that they had lost heart with the affairs of men. So I knew that other gods had our concerns in hand. From them my Power must come. They were more patient than these, it may be, more understanding of the terrible limitations of the body that shackled our minds and spirits.

With a wrenching eddy, the wind removed me from the place, if place it was. I found myself suspended in a colorless nothingness that made the blank fields of snow across which we had journeyed seem places a-teem with color and life.

Time disappeared from me; all sense of selfhood was lost

amid that blot of space in the fabric of being. All that was left to me was the little spark that had been "I" since the day I first looked upon the world and knew that I existed. How much that self had depended upon its surroundings as yardsticks for measuring itself I had not truly known. Now, with no thing or person to try it against, I was left to contemplate it as if it were no part of me.

It seemed that I hung motionless in that unknown dimension for a span of lifetimes. I sifted through my own soul, atom by atom, and what I found was less than I had hoped. It was, however, more that I had feared it might be. I learned my faults . . . and I knew that I could deal with them, now that I knew their faces. I pried, tremblingly, into my weaknesses. They were many. Those I knew that I must conquer, one at a time, as time and circumstances brought them to trial.

To my comfort, I found that I was not deceived in my strengths. The toughness and tenacity, the capacities for anger and innovation that I had known to be a part of me were shown to be useful things, not the faults that my teachers had seemed to think them. Yet even that knowledge did not lessen my pain.

I drew away, sickened with so much knowledge of things that the gods mercifully hide from us. And the wind drew me softly away.

I opened my eyes, and the whiteness of the light coming through our breathing hole told me that dawn had passed. I turned my head, to find the dark and sorrowful eyes of the Beast regarding me. From beyond her furry body, Lisaux said, "I had not hoped to rest so well and warmly. Once again, we owe thanks to our Beast."

Without answering his remark, I said, "Lisaux, did you dream?"

He grunted, "I cannot remember, Singer, though it seems to me that I was in a place all gray with mists . . ." his voice died away as he strained to recall his vision.

The Beast squirmed about until she could stand, then looked down at me and gave a strange cry. Soft as it was, it carried the weight of both affirmation and urgency.

We rose at once, Lisaux and I, rolled our blankets away tightly into our packs, munched a bit of mush cake that had been dotted with dried fruit and nuts, and went out into the snow. Again, the sun was rising clear over the distant line that marked the escarpment. We looked southward, and the spur toward which we had moved rose sharp and clear in the cold air, its eastward side rosy, its westward one purple with shadow.

"We must go . . . there?" murmured Lisaux, knitting his brows.

"You had the same dream—or something of the same experience—as I did," I said. "We must go there. For what reason, I do not know. But there."

We set out, the Beast leading, as if in her impatience she could not stay behind. The rest had put new life into our limbs, and we moved at a goodly clip, using her broken trail to best advantage. Thus, we finally began to draw near to that soaring tooth of rock, finding that it was taller and broader than we had suspected.

As we came nearer to it, we found that Plain was studded with snow-covered obstacles that proved to be boulders as large as farmers' cottages. Closer in, they were more numerous, and we could see that the foot of the spire was jumbled with even larger stones, tossed there as if by a giant child weary of his toys.

Then, between one step and the next, the outline of the spur wavered. The boulders at its foot vanished in mist. The air about us grew warmer, though the snow beneath our boots was not melting.

"Hold fast together!" I cried, as I felt the familiar gray miasma fold about us. Then those tenuous walls were there.

We stood opposite the door of my dream.

We looked at one another. "Yesss," breathed Lisaux. He went to the door with the confidence of familiarity. It opened to him easily, and we entered, first Lisaux, then I, then the Beast. The garden was as I remembered it, aswirl with mists. The fountain played its bright games in the center, but the door opposite our entryway was closed.

As we crossed the garden, I expected to feel again the curiosity of the shadow figures that had been there before. The place was empty of all save the mist and the fountain's light. Before the door as we approached lay a bar of deepest shade.

Lisaux made as if to set his foot upon that dark strip. Then he hesitated, as though some inner warning had sounded. I moved beside him and looked down. The Beast came to stand between us. She also regarded that simple shadow with suspicion.

It lay there; through it we could see the spongy turf of the garden, the occasional pebble. Yet I felt as if I stood at the edge of an abyss that dwarfed the escarpment to the east. A deep mystery was there, and I felt that it was a test laid before us by those who summoned us here.

I stooped and groped for a pebble, which I held loosely and tossed into the bar of darkness. It winked from view. No trace of it appeared on the ground that seemed to lie within the shadow.

Lisaux drew forth the black blade. "This weapon has been blessed," he said, "by those most holy to us of Malchion. It bears the weight of many prayers and of just deeds. Never has it been used in an unjust cause. I will take risk of its loss, in this time and place, for I feel that beyond that door lies much that we must know before going on our way. It would be better to go weaponless into the south than to turn aside from the mysteries that have brought us to this door."

With that, he laid the dark blade across the equally dark shadow, bridging that line from our feet to the doorsill. There came a flash of stunning brightness. The sword seemed to grow before our eyes into a firm and shining pathway.

Lisaux stepped forward, set his feet upon that way, and reached the door, which opened before him. I followed, a bit hesitantly. Those who are adept tend to distrust any magics not their own. But the path of the sword was firm underfoot, and I soon stood within that bright hall where the Gray Sisters had sat. The Beast, at my heels, breathed against my neck as she looked over my shoulder into the curving chamber, where the blaze on the hearth had died to a glimmer.

The tall chairs were pushed back from the hearth and sat empty. There was no sound within the hall, no breath of presence. Nonplussed, we stood quietly in the doorway, waiting for some signal that our presence was noted.

In the warmth of that other-dimensional place, my fur garments were torture. I slipped my cloak and over-tunic to the floor, then sat on them to remove my fur boots. Lisaux grunted and began to do the same.

"I dreamed of this place," he said. "Was that your dream, also?"

I nodded, and he continued, "I won my way across that garden out there with my blade drawn and busy, though no drop of blood was spilled from any who barred my passage. When I came through the door, there were three tall women here, all in gray. They said to me, 'Even so must one who walks blindly in the ways of the gods use his skills and his wits.' Then I was borne away by a wind, and I can remember nothing else."

"I wonder," I said, "where those Gray Sisters might be. They have summoned us here, with much effort. They have more to say to us, of that I am certain."

As if in answer, there was a stir upon the stair that curved away up the wall to our left. Three quiverings of mist spun there, curdling into shapes like those I had seen in my dream. They ceased to whirl, stood for a moment regarding us with those remarkable eyes, and moved smoothly down the steps toward us.

"So you come, Children of Flesh, to our call yet again. We have given each of you a dream that has taught you much. You, Singer, recall the whole of yours, for so you are trained to do. You, Warrior, recall little of yours, now . . . but the rest will come to you at need. You, Beast of the Snows, knew much that we showed you before we ever met. To you we give honor, for yours is a task that would give pause even to those of us of the family of the gods." The voice drifted over us, quiet and musical. From which of the three it came, I was unable to discover.

Lisaux sank to one knee and bowed his head. "I had never thought to look with my living eyes upon the faces of any of the gods," he said.

The Beast walked past me to the foot of the stair, waiting until the three reached her. Then she looked up into their eyes. All stood in a moment of frozen silence.

When they moved, I also went forward and bowed my own head. Not for long, for it is not in my nature to give the outward signs of reverence. "I have learned the lessons you set me, Sisters of the gods," I said. "How they may help in the work I attempt, I cannot yet know. Yet I must thank you for showing me the way to look into my own heart and the hearts of my fellows. Thank you for forcing me to examine my own motives. I am, perhaps, the weakest staff upon which your kindred might have chosen to rest the weight of their purpose."

The tallest, in the center, looked down at me from her superior height. There was laughter in those clear and shining eyes as she said, "Let humility sink less deeply into your soul, small sister. You will need arrogance and confidence in what you do. The minds of those of our kindred whom you serve are not open to us, but we know one thing surely: None in the south of Tyrnos will look for their reckoning to come at the hands of one so unassuming as yourself. Small, gentle people they tend to ignore as unimportant to their great affairs, which is one reason, no doubt, that our kin chose you for the task."

Now they had all three come to stand with their backs to the little flicker of fire that still lived on their hearth. The laughter was gone from the eyes of the tallest. It had never been in those of her Sisters. They stood, as tall and stern and frightening as the gods they were, the fire behind them wakening into roaring life.

"We have taken little note, for aeons beyond counting, of the doings of your folk," they said in one calm and chilling voice. "That is a fault, we now see, for we have left all to our kin, losing ourselves in the motions of growth and weather and such simple things.

"Now we have waked from our folly. We cannot, at this time, take your affairs in hand. By so doing we might well disturb the workings of our fellows. Yet we can oversee what passes over all Tyrnos and the world that contains it and many worlds beside.

"Your hearts are sound; that we have determined for ourselves. Yet you are beings of terrible fallibility. An unwise decision at a moment of stress or deception, a faltering of courage and will, could deliver Tyrnos, as well as Riahith itself, into the hands of the Ethrans, whom we know of old. We wish you nothing but good, but we will not allow your errors to endanger this planet into which we have poured so much care and love. We have lived here since it has held soil and air and water with which to nourish life.

"We will destroy you, if it seems wise to us."

# 13

## *The Hut in the Snow*

WITH those words, the hall, the fire, the Sisters winked out of existence. We found ourselves standing at the foot of that ominous spur of rock, tugging on our furs and our boots amid thigh-deep snow. The sun had moved little from its former position when the walls appeared to us, and we were relieved to find the forenoon still with us.

Now Lisaux looked at me with puzzled eyes. "I think we have been ensorcelled, Singer," he said. "We forgot the last of our enemies, though he must be nearby. The Holdorn said that his shepherd's hut lies below this rock we followed from the north.

"When we left Holdorn, we were in great haste to attend to this villain, then to hasten southward. We forgot much of our errand."

"We were not led away from our errand," I answered. "We were led more deeply into it and given a warning that we must hold in heart. Now we have remembered what must be done, the time and the place being again together, though I think we would not have been allowed to forget completely."

With that, we looked to the Beast. She lifted her nose into the faint, chill breeze that moved over the snow. Then she set off, moving around the spur on its westward side. We crunched wearily after her through the half-frozen snow, my short legs rapidly wearing to numb-kneed stumbling.

Lisaux, sensing my distress, began to drag his feet, making a trench of the Beast's clear trail. I walked more easily then, able to look about, as well as to feel abroad with the odd sensitivities that seemed to be growing in me. Against my back, the spot where the "house" of the Gray Sisters had stood radiated a sort of burning chill, an excitation of the nerves that lessened with dreadful slowness as we drew away. Only when the spur lay between was I able to forget it and to find the faint tingle that meant the presence of another human being.

It seemed that the attributes I had assumed in my "dream" had clung to me. When I sensed that life ahead in the snow, I knew that it was not that of the man we sought. This was a strong and simple life, gnarled and honest as the rock behind us.

As the Beast led us forward, I realized that her path was curving more to the south, missing the spot where one of our kind drew breath. Touching Lisaux on the shoulder, I gestured to our left.

"One is there, and it is not the one we seek."

The Beast caught my words as she loped back through the snow to find the cause of our hesitation. As if embarrassed, she lifted her short nose to the breeze, sniffed deeply, then moved away toward the spot where I felt that spark of life.

The shepherd had rooted out a shelter in the snow, much as the Beast had done, in the lee of one of the giant boulders. Lacking strength to forage for fuel, and being blessed with a shelter that would have melted, she had found or called up two sheep and placed them in her haven. Then she had gone to earth between their tethered bodies and left it to the gods to send help for her terrible wounds.

She must have fought the escaping villain with stubborn courage. The staff beside her hand was splintered short and stained with blood. She was gaunt and tough and wrinkled as desert thorn, we found when we moved the sheep and knelt beside her. The stab through her shoulder muscle had clotted on both sides and seemed not so ill, but the slash across her ribcage opened and closed with every breath. If it had been summer, it would have gone badly with her; but the cold had been her friend. The gash had not mortified, though it oozed pale blood at every inhalation.

We had been so long together, by now, that Lisaux and the Beast and I knew without words what each must do. I opened the sheepskin cloak and unfastened the strings of the rough woollen garment she wore, while Lisaux rummaged in his pack for our herbs and ointments. The Beast waited beside me, patient and knowing, until I had the wounds free of cloth. Then she carefully and thoroughly licked them clean.

When we had anointed the shepherdess and wrapped her in bandages and both our fur rugs, we knew that she must have better shelter than this, and soon. There was only one such nearby. We knew that it must be tenanted by our old enemy, so we went again to the southward after the scent of our prey, leaving our patient secure for the time.

We smelled the heavy peat smoke long before the low and rounded shape of the mud-walled hut came into view. We separated, the Beast taking the long way round to the farther side, Lisaux taking the northeast, and I walking straight to the door. It was a layered sheepskin affair, and I waited until my companions were in position before reaching forward with my walking staff and sweeping the hangings aside with one swift motion.

He was lying on the woolly rug before the smoky fire. A more battered face I had never seen, as he spasmed upright and glared about in startled desperation. Lisaux's solid shape showed through the parchment of the one small window, and the Beast's purr reverberated round and round the entire hut.

He was tall, broad, far stronger than I, but I had no fear of him. The shepherd woman had done her work well. He would never again attack confidently just because his prey was female. I could see by the set of his head and the tension of his shoulders that he was wary of me and terrified of my companions. When I eased my blade back into its sheath, he dropped onto a low stool and drew a shuddering breath. It was easy to read him. He had been living in dread of this moment since his escape from Holdorn.

Lisaux was now behind me. I moved forward into the low and smoky room. When the Beast followed us, there was scarcely room to move. We stood uncomfortably, looking down at the man we had sought. Lisaux, head bent to avoid brushing the low ceiling, was pale and grim. The Beast kept lifting the corner of her lip in a silent snarl.

I, however, had succeeded, as a Singer must, in subduing my anger and disgust. With a gesture toward my companions, I said, "We have followed you far. Yet none of us knows your name. How did they call you, those lost comrades of yours?"

"All dead?" he whispered. "Ruif, I knew, and Lach, and Gron, but Garz was alive . . ."

"Until whoever gave to him the blue-stone symbol sent from afar to extract payment for it," I finished for him. "He died in pain, and the symbol was written in mist over his agony. Before he died, he told us of the visitor to Eruifal. Have you the mate to his medallion?"

He fumbled in his tunic and drew out the twin to Garz's. "Ruif gave me this, saying that it was license from those who are masters of the world. 'Andri,' he said to me, 'this will give us leave to go back to the old times, when we took without payment and gave nothing to man or to the gods.' " His throat worked as I made to hand the thing back to him. He gestured it away with a frantic thrust of his hand.

"It gave us nothing that we truly wanted. We walked, most times, in a haze and a fog, scarce knowing what we did. Our sins gave us no pleasure. Gold bought nothing we desired. I felt, at times, as though some grinning *thing* peered over my shoulder, urging me on to do things I had never thought of doing before. Take it! I want none of it!"

I smiled grimly and held the thing high, letting the dull chain swing until the medallion spun, a blur of blue and tarnished bronze. A note rose in my throat. I opened my mouth and let it grow to fill the hut with its deep tone. The *Huym* spun faster, and the blur became a circle of gray that seemed to be a window into . . . elsewhere.

A face grew there, in the gray. Oval, ivory-skinned, violet-eyed, it looked out of the blur. The mouth moved, but no words could be distinguished. I knew that face. Its likeness was stamped into the ivory plaque that centered the Singing Wall of my school and that of all such Schools in Tyrnos. Ahlia, Singer to the High King, administrator of the Order, looked out into the shepherd's hut, and I could see that that clear-cut face had lost its pristine quality.

A frown grew between the arched brows. A question formed on the lips, whose curve was no longer good-tempered. She knew, I understood well, that someone observed her through the use of Power. Yet she could not see us. The restless, searching movements of her eyes said that. Doubtless, the question was, "Who dares to observe *me*, unsummoned?"

I let the spinning slow; the gray thinned, became again blue and bronze. The face was gone like smoke, and I looked into Lisaux's eyes.

"She is the head of my Order. The foremost Singer of Tyrnos. The keeper of the conscience of the High King."

He nodded. "It explains much," he said, taking the thing from my hand. The peat fire was smoky, and there was little glow in the center, but there he laid the *Huym*. It lay there, rippling with heat, as it grew hotter. When the stones melted, at last, the entire thing crumbled into powder. The tiny room felt cleaner at once.

There was a gasp from our prisoner. He had gone chalky

pale. The bruises that the shepherd had laid across his cheek-bones were like protuberant blots against his pallor. His eyes seemed to be turning inward, and I could feel the beginning of the sick miasma that had hung in the room where Garz had died.

I did not intend to have another captive snatched away from my custody. Inhaling deeply for ten breaths, I called upon the Power. It channelled into me with overwhelming force, and I sang an ascending sequence of notes that crescendoed into volume fit to shake the walls. The ashes of the medallion shrank upon themselves, and the greenish fog lightened in color. Lisaux and the Beast were upon their knees; the man's hands were over his ears; and the Beast had her head burrowed into his cloak to dull the sound.

With deliberation, the music bursting from my throat retraced the scale it had ascended, with vibrations quavering about each of the notes as it slowed and quieted. The mist thinned still further. Then it was gone. The last note rang triumphantly about the mud-walled room.

Then I knelt beside the man and touched his face. He breathed. His color was returning. I had acted in time, before the terrible death of Garz had overtaken him. I eased his slumped form onto the sheepskin rug and turned to see to Lisaux.

He was rising to his feet, a sheepish expression on his face. "I had not yet heard the extent of the Power you can summon, Lady," he said. "The ears of common men are not attuned to such potencies. My skull was fit to burst with your music."

The Beast came to my side and rubbed her chin against my shoulder. Her purr rumbled in her chest, and I knew that she both understood and approved of what I had done. Together, we looked down at the man on the rug. Though he had acted with his fellows in the commission of vile crimes, we felt now that he was not wholly guilty. Even Lisaux's face held a trace of pity.

"Leeana said to me, while you slept, Singer, that it was her intuition that her abductors were not wholly under their own control. Even Ruif, who understood more of whatever unholy pact the Ethran brought to him, was compelled, I know now. Only his long fixation upon my wife gave him the strength to follow his own wishes and carry out her abduction. Much has been clarified by the words of Garz and Andri." He bent and lifted Andri and bore him to the pile of skins against the back wall.

The Beast growled gruffly beside the door. My companion shrugged his cloak about him and said, "I must go after the woman in the snow. There is no need for you to struggle through the drifts again. Build up the fire . . . I will bring her quickly."

I nodded and turned to the pile of peat beside the hearth, placing bits carefully on the smudge of glowing coal. Soon there was a fair blaze, though the hut became more smoky by the moment. I slid the doorskins aside to let the chill air swirl through the room.

The door opened to the west, and the sun was midway down the visible arc of sky. Only a step brought me to a point from which I could see the rock that loomed over the hut. Lisaux and the Beast were not to be seen, for snow-mounded stones lay all about, so I raised my eyes to the pinnacle of the stone spur.

My breath caught in my throat. The full gaze of the sun shone upon the sharp tooth that spired upward from the jagged top. At the tip of the spire was a dazzle of light that defied the penetration of my eyes. But my heart told me that an enemy existed within that sharp glare . . . an enemy who must not know of our presence here.

Lisaux's mind was all but closed to me, I knew from past

experience. The Beast, however, was a sister spirit. Toward her I sent a desperate appeal: *Warn Lisaux to conceal himself from the peak!*

Across the chill space, I felt a surge of affirmation. I drew a deep breath of relief. Upon that peak, I felt certain, was some device or weapon of the Ethrans. My own sort had no need of devices of metal and glass, so far as I knew, but I remembered the Ethran's house and his tower, filled with unnameable things. I surmised that his brothers were likewise armed with strange weapons.

A sudden thought surprised me as I stepped back into the hut. Young as I was as a Singer, only an initiate of the third order, I had not had complete training in the techniques and devices that the great adepts of my kind might command, but I had delved, unbidden and unwelcomed, into such lore as deeply as my teachers would permit. Those investigations had hinted at much more than they had revealed. I knew enough of the capabilities of such things to shudder at the possibilities.

Ahlia was the Mother of us all, we had been taught, subject only to the gods. In direct lineage, she traced her ancestry and her training into the depths of antiquity, to the original Ahlia, first and greatest Soul-Singer of Tyrnos. Now I had roused her attention with my childish games with the medallion. What might I have brought upon us as a result?

I felt a sudden frantic need for motion. As soon as possible, I knew that we must flee southward from this place.

# 14

## *The Dancing of the Beast*

WELL before sundown Lisaux returned with the shepherd, and we tended her carefully, managing to slip broth and crumbled bread into her, though she was not conscious of it. Our prisoner moved apathetically. It seemed almost as if, with the removal of the medallion, his volition had also been lost.

The compulsion that I had felt before was now becoming irresistible. The demeanor of the captive suggested a thought to me. I lost no time in asking Lisaux, "What would you think of leaving her in the care of Andri? He cannot escape. Even without the snow, I think he has lost the will and the wit to flee. I can set a kind of spell upon him that will hold for many days. In that time, the Holdorn and his sons, if not more, will come in our track.

"They will see the woman safely to Holdorn before following us; they will attend to Andri. Our own duty lies elsewhere; I feel urgently that we should move under the hem of night into the snowfields and across them. When the sun rises again, we need to be far from this place and under the shelter of trees again. Something is upon yonder peak that is searching for us."

Lisaux stepped to the door, pushing aside the skins. The last ray from the sun lanced across space to strike the rock above us. That uncanny sparkle glinted an evil tint, reddened by the setting sun. The air held a tension that set my neck hairs a-crawl. I could see that Lisaux felt something of the same apprehension.

We stepped back into the hut and closed the hangings.

"Set your spell," he grunted. "There is something abroad that means us ill, without doubt. If we are to move at all, it must be done tonight. That red glare means death. I am an old friend of death, and I recognize him at a distance." He laughed grimly.

I moved to Andri's side and shook him to alertness. "We must go," I told him. "You must remain here and care for this woman whom you have hurt. If you do it well and carefully, those who follow us will deal less harshly with you.

"Do not leave the hut in daylight. There is danger about, though I believe that it will follow Lisaux and the Beast and me when we go. Still, you should take all care to stay indoors by day until help comes.

"I am going to sing you a song . . ." and I began to hum. The binding song is a strange one, not brought forth with Power as so many of our musics are, but spun like a web, strand over strand over strand of repetitive melody, hypnotic and soothing.

When he was well enmeshed, I wound the humming down, slowly and gently, that the thread of suggestion might not snap. Then I repeated my orders, and he parroted them back with the bright docility of a child.

While I was at my task, Lisaux had made a hot and appetizing meal for us. I saw that the great pot of meat-thick stew would last until Andri found wit enough to make more. We ate on the stone hearth, soaking in the heat of the slow peat fire as we did so.

When our meal was done, we donned our furs again, shrugged on our heavy packs, and approached the door.

Though the fire was again low, we knew that no glimmer of
it must betray our departure. First I held the inner sheepskins
while Lisaux worked his way between them and the outer
ones. Then I pushed them tightly against the mud wall while
he moved through the outermost layers. Then we reversed
the process as I went through. We were satisfied that no hint
of firelight had slivered across the snow to alert whatever
watched above.

The Beast moved ahead again, leading us rapidly southward, bearing always slightly to the east. The rock behind us,
I saw from time to time, was dwindling, its bulk against the
starry sky growing smaller at each backward glance. No hint
of brightness glinted at its peak, and I had no intuition of
danger.

When we had traveled for over an hour, I whispered to
Lisaux, "Do you think those we left will be in any danger?"

He did not turn but grunted in return, "My heart is heavy
that we must leave them there, one all but witless and the
other unconscious. Yet what could we do? We could not have
brought the woman out into the cold again, and Andri was
the only one to stay and care for her.

"Still, all my instincts tell me that you are the one who is
hunted. Your hand held the medallion. Your voice sang the
note that brought the face of Ahlia. That thing aloft, if it is
Ethran, is probably one that can be focused upon specific
prey. What would it profit those in the Citadel to send blind
forces about to slay indiscriminately?"

His words comforted me with their logic. I looked back no
more, setting my whole strength to holding the pace my companions set. That was no easy task, itself, for one had four
legs and the other two that were far longer than mine. Had
they not broken the trail for me, I would have been sore put to
keep up with them.

The night wore on, and the sky, so clear to begin, had an

edge of cloud to the west. By the time we had moved under the lip of the high ground again, there was a hint of light above its eastern rim.

It was now no escarpment, merely a long ridge of higher country that cut from north to south, curving inward to meet the hills that marked the southern end of the range of low mountains at the west of the Sunken Plain. Where the two met in a jumble of rock and hillocks, we climbed up and out of the Plain. As we climbed, day moved up behind the clouds that now hung thickly overhead.

We reached the top amid a spatter of snow that whirled lazily down the windless sky. For almost a league, the country lay before us in treeless undulations. And now I felt again the tang of danger cutting through me more fiercely than a cold wind. Although no sun could strike it to brightness, I felt the nearness of that thing that had been above the shepherd's hut.

Lisaux felt it too. He gestured to me, and we slipped back down the slope to huddle among the snowy maze of rocks below the ridge. We hastily plastered our cloaks with more snow, to make ourselves hard to see. As we worked, the Beast crept close and laid her head on my shoulder.

I stopped and looked into her eyes. There was no message there . . . for me. From her came a feeling so eery and so fey that I was caught up in it, for a moment. She rubbed her whiskers against my cloaked arm, then she moved and did the same to Lisaux. Her purr rumbled forth as she slipped effortlessly up the ridge and emerged onto the lip above us.

The air was now thick with snow and also with impending and indefinable things. Without a word, Lisaux and I wriggled to a point from which we could see the Beast as she stood looking back across the Plain.

We turned our heads. At first, it seemed that a thicker squall of snow whirled toward us. Then we saw that it was something else. A whirl of bright flecks danced across the

gray-white air, homing upon the gazing Beast. As it drew
near, it rose higher and higher. When it reached a point just
above her, it stopped its forward motion and spun madly two
man-heights over her head.

Her purr boomed out, seeming to make the very rock beneath our bellies reverberate. She looked up into the spiral
of flecks and stretched, catlike, switching her short tail with
its snowy fringe. Then she rose delicately to the tips of her
clawed toes and began to dance.

As she did not sing as men do, so she did not dance as they
do. Her lithe body shaped itself on the earth and in the air,
flowing from one pattern to the next with inevitable grace
and a meaning that spoke to the muscles and the inward parts,
not to the conscious mind. Her feet missed no phrase of the
inaudible music to which she moved. They traced a slow circle about the spot over which the thing hovered, but so ab-
sorbing was her motion that no one untrained in such matters
would have noticed what she was about.

Three times she circled, the steps falling neatly into place.
Her curving body, her gesturing paws decorated the pattern
with flourishes, and her tail kept the time with perfect
rhythm. The statement that was her dance rounded upon itself and drew to an ending. The thing that spun above her
twinkled changelessly.

At the last, the Beast stood upright, just below it. With a
languid gesture, she swept one paw upward and down. The
device followed it, its lazy sparkles changing to a desperate
glittering.

Lisaux and I swarmed up the slope and moved almost to the
edge of the circle of pawprints. The Beast had placed the
thing in the exact center of the pattern she had woven. It lay
there rippling with light that spoke of frustration and anger.
But her magics, whatever sort they might have been, held fast,
and it could not move.

With one spring, she leaped outside the trap, leaving not

one mark in the snow to spoil the symmetry. She sagged wearily against me, and without a glance at our erstwhile pursuer, we half lifted her and bore her away toward the distant line of trees that hemmed the snowfield before us.

Once we stopped to rest, and I looked back. An unholy brightness marked the place where our pursuer was imprisoned. The light was pulsing as if with effort. I surmised that the thing was gifted with a certain amount of will and intelligence, though I avoided the thought that it might be a sort of sentient creature. Still, that struggling of the thing in its web of entrapment stayed with me as we moved on.

The Beast was heavy. She was fully as large as Lisaux, though her long thin legs and strange proportions made her look fragile and light. In the deep snow, we expended much effort, but we felt compelled to hide ourselves, so we plodded on. By the time we reached the outer fringe of young trees, we were so exhausted that we dropped both the Beast and ourselves under the first passably thick batch of bushes and covered ourselves, over and under, with the blankets.

The quiet, windless snow continued to fall, lying so lightly that it would pile up a finger's length atop a twig before its own weight toppled it. This pleased us, for our tracks were soon covered, as well as our sheltering thicket.

Now came our turn to warm the Beast, whose furry body had so often performed the same task for us. We turned to her and wrapped our arms about her, Lisaux on one side and I on the other. Our exertions in the snow had set our blood racing, and we generated warmth beneath our fur coverings sufficient to penetrate our garments and reach the Beast. After a time, as the sky grew darker with both snow cloud and the coming night, she relaxed into sound sleep. Then her own system began to generate heat in place of the deadly chill that had wrapped her, after her dance.

We all slept, without caution and without dream, as the night and the snow fell together.

We woke together in a profound darkness. The compulsion to flee was hard upon us all, and I wondered if the strength of the spell that held the thing was beginning to wane. However it might be, there was no sleep left in us. We ate a bit, the Beast consenting to gulp a bit of our dried meat. Then we moved away into the blackness.

Lisaux had a fine sense of direction. I was able to call upon a bit of the Power to direct me. Neither gift was needed, for the Beast knew unerringly the way that we must go. Whether she had roamed these lands before or simply had an animal's ability to read invisible paths by scent and instinct, I cannot tell. However it was, she skirted copses that would have hindered us. She avoided deep pools that we would have thought to be smooth stretches of snow, if she had not warned us. Taking us by the quickest and most direct route, she led us through the scattered forest that stretched for seemingly endless leagues.

Always, I felt a probing and a searching moving through the lands we crossed. Perhaps it was the device, freed from its captivity but still befuddled by the magic. More likely, it was the mind of Ahlia, stirred from its complacency by my ill-advised use of the medallion. The abilities at her command were many and frightening, I knew. Still, there were musics for every need in a Singer's repertory, and I hummed a hiding tune, a very small one unlikely to cause ripples that might rouse the interest of adepts.

So we crossed the wooded leagues, and when morning was lighting the east, we found ourselves in a forest so old and so great that it made the mang-tree wood seem a patch of saplings by contrast. The trees were of a kind that I had never seen, though I recognized and named them. We were taught many things at our School besides singing.

"Orhan," I said to Lisaux, gesturing upward. "The oldest trees that now stand upon the globe of Riahith. They lived when our fathers still grubbed for roots and hunted beetles for their food. I would guess that only the Gray Sisters could count their age. This is a wood so full of old magics and lost memories that even Singers hesitate to enter it. Those who taught us its lore rushed headlong through the tale, and none of our questions concerning it were answered.

He looked about and nodded slowly. We stood in an enchanted place. The giant boles stood well apart with only their extended branch tips touching to make a continuous roof over the forest floor. That floor was carpeted with snow, so smoothly carpeted that one could see that no undergrowth or deadfall lay beneath it. The trees were every shade of gray, and like the Gray Sisters' garb, their sober shades held unobtrusive colors.

A feathery snow was falling, its great clotted flakes wandering quietly downward through the lace of barren twigs. It draped the wood in a veiling that gave an other-worldly mood to the day and the spot where we stood. The reaches that stretched away into the deeps of the forest dissolved, at the edge of seeing, into a mist of white-gray that seemed to hide secrets best left unrevealed.

The Beast raised her head, her gray-fringed ears twitching forward, and looked into the depths of the mysteries that lay there. Then, without turning to see if we followed, she stepped deliberately away, toward the south, the heart of Orhan Forest, and the uneasy deeps of the wood.

I sighed. It seemed so simple, now, the doing of the tasks I had done before. Razul seemed only mildly villainous and his retribution the play of a child, in the light of my recent adventures and discoveries. Lisaux, too, took a deep breath and shrugged his pack irritably. High moods of mysticism are all very well and stimulating to the spirit, but they wear one to the bone when unleavened by laughter and hot meals and dry, warm beds. Even a Singer must vary her diet of stresses and Powers with intervals of plain humanity, else she would go mad or wear away entirely.

Our Beast, however, lived upon a level of existence all but inaccessible to us. Unceasing effort, unwavering attention were a constant state with her. I wondered, as we crunched through the snow in her track, what manner of being she truly was. The Bestiaries of the School held no mention of her kind, I was certain, for they had been my delight in the long evenings when we had an hour of freedom.

She had seemed to be, in some way, attuned to the Gray Sisters. I mused upon that for a time. Then I dismissed the thought. The gods were strange and unpredictable at times, but surely they would not take upon themselves the guise of an animal, however wise and faithful. It was a hopeless puzzle, and I put it from my mind and moved close behind Lisaux.

"What, I wonder, did the Ethran hope to gain in shackling those of Eruifal to its purposes?" I asked his snow-dusted back. "Surely, it was of no interest to it whether Leeana was or was not in her home. I feel that Ruif added her to the equation of his own will. How think you?"

I could see the slow nod of his hooded head. His voice floated back to me, quiet but clear in the snow-stillness. "I believe that to be true," he said. "It may be that there are Ethrans in all the lands of Riahith. I have given much thought to this problem, and it seems to my judgment that they may well be engaged in an attempt to disrupt every government and to hold sway over all people in our world. Malchion is so near to Tyrnos that one Ethran might well do the work of two.

"It was simply ill-fortune for the Ethran that Ruif was besotted with lust for my wife. It was doubly unlucky for him that Ruif waked from his bemusement enough to realize that neither walls nor weapons nor death itself could hold me from his throat, after he had abducted her. The flight into Tyrnos was no plot of anyone's, I'll be bound, but the reflex of a frightened man who valued his worthless life. It may be that in involving Eruifal, which in turn involved me, which brought me to you, those who work evil in our lands have overstepped themselves."

It was my turn to nod. Leeana had been right. Lisaux was a man of direct and forceful mind, as well as subtle understanding. Though I had thought upon the same ground, he had set it all logically in order so that one might trace cause and effect as if they were mapped upon a chart.

"You have left out one thing," I said to him, after a time. "The gods move men to their wills, not only when our need and desperation call, but also when we neither know nor expect it. I am not convinced that they might not also move Ethrans, even if those gray folk have no belief in the powers of either gods or men."

But Lisaux made no answer. He stopped in his tracks, and I almost drove my nose into his back before I knew he had ceased to walk.

Ahead of us, the Beast was moving back along her trail toward us. She had a wide grin on her furry face, and her walk was almost a gambol. Her purr sounded through the wide wood as if a hive of gigantic bees had been thumped with a stone.

Behind her in the white distance we could see a dark figure that seemed to be sitting upon a log or a stone. As the Beast reached us, that figure rose and held out its hands, beckoning.

A compulsion unlike any I have ever felt before rose in me. I hurried forward, knowing that Lisaux was doing the same.

# 15

## *The One Who Watches All*

WE found, as we neared that waiting shape, that the snow was deeper than any we had crossed since beginning our trek through the wood. Foundering and gasping, we shed our packs and struggled on, and the dark and slender one waited, hands still extended, until we stood face to face. Yet not quite that, for the being was far taller even than Lisaux. It towered above me, and the Beast wove about its knees like a housecat.

When it lowered its hands, we found that compulsion lifted from our hearts. We looked at one another with desperate speculation, then turned to the one before us, waiting. The Beast sensed our unease and moved to stand between us, her purr rumbling again in the still air.

It was none of our own kind that we faced, nor yet was it an Ethran. Unlike the Gray Sisters, it was nevertheless somewhat reminiscent of them in its air of total confidence. Its hood's peak almost touched the lowest bough of the giant tree under which it stood. Its robe flowed downward from that point to puddle about its invisible feet. The face that peered interestedly from the depths of that black hood was one to snare one's mind.

It was an old face, tracked with time as a mountain is tracked with weather. Its eyes were black and bright and sharp, glinting brightly through the misty air of the forest. It was neither male nor female. No sense of gender emanated from it at all, but one felt no lack. Instead, there was a feeling of keen mind and overriding personhood that left me, at the least, a bit intimidated.

Lisaux, however, was a different story. I remembered with relief that he was much older and, in the ways of the world, infinitely wiser than I. The veteran of battles and court intrigues, he stood confidently before this strange observer in the midst of an enchanted wood and stared it up and down.

Without arrogance, but with utmost confidence, he asked, "Who are you who summon us through the snow? The Beast's demeanor assures us that you are no enemy, but are you, indeed, a friend?"

The wrinkled face cracked into a thousand-creased smile. The black eyes flicked up and down us both before it spoke. Then it said, "I am Enderon, the Watcher. For millennia, I have sat in the forest and observed the winds and the waters, the cycling of seasons, the oddities of beast and bird and humankind. Those who have met me here have run away, if they ran upon two legs. The four-legged and winged ones have learned that I can be a friend, if they have need and the fortitude to withstand my gaze."

Now I began to understand. Among the oldest lore of Tyrnos is a tale of the One Who Watches All. A living myth stood before us.

Taking courage, I asked, "Do you see afar, Wise One, or is your vision limited to the ways of the wood?"

Those eyes stabbed into me for a moment, then it said, "Once, I saw across all the lands and the mountains and even the seas beyond the mountains. I sickened, as men grew grasping and mindlessly cruel. So I withdrew my sight, by league and by league, until it moved within Orhan. I look abroad no more, unless dire need calls me."

"It may be that we bring the voice of that need," I said.

"Hear our tale. Then, if you will, give us your thought."

So we told Enderon of our task. First Lisaux told of his desperate pursuit of his wife and those who had stolen her away, of his time of suspension in the Ethran's house and his meeting with me. When he had done, I took up the tale, beginning far back with my injury on the road. I told of Kalir and the fate of Razul, of Rellas's detention in the Citadel, and all that had happened in the mang forest. Then, by turns, we told of our questing and its results.

When I described the face that had appeared in the circle of gray, Enderon gave a start and bent down until its wrinkled face was level with my own, looking into my eyes.

"Ahlia is known to me, and her ancestors also. As each takes up the task of governing the Singers, I look upon him or her, examine the heart and the mind, making certain that the task is held in capable hands. She was strong, this Ahlia, and of good intention."

"We believe," interjected Lisaux, "that the Ethrans are corrupting our world. By means of devices, as I know to my cost, they can alter the conditions of Humankind. They can seal the body and the mind into stasis. They can alter the thinking of those who make bond with them. This we have seen for ourselves. It is our thought that they have in some subtle way insinuated themselves into the confidence of the High King. That would lead inevitably to their meeting with and entrapping the spirit of his Singer. It is easy to corrupt a kingdom if one begins at the pinnacle of power."

The black eyes glittered angrily. "I have seen it many times," Enderon hissed. "Yet never has this wickedness come from those who have no root in the soil of Riahith. I have been remiss, I can see. Looking only to my own comfortable boundaries, I have allowed forces from outside to penetrate the world without my knowing it. Upon my head is much of the sorrow you have seen. I am the warden set by the gods. They have given me power to use as I find the need, and it may well be that if I had seen the Ethrans come, I could have removed them from Riahith before they could work harm. You bring me sore tidings!"

It stood, head bent, arms folded as if to ward off the cold, with anguish radiating from its shape. The Beast, always sensitive to pain, rubbed her head against Enderon's knees. This brought that weird being to itself, and it sank upon the stone, bringing its face to our level.

"We must look into the Citadel," Enderon said. "Your vision must accompany mine, for you may see things among your own kind that I might overlook. But this is not the place for such traveling. My body is imperishable. Yours are not, and we must leave them in safety, guarded by yonder Beast, while we seek southward."

Again it rose. This time it moved away into the forest, and we followed . . . not in its track, for it made none. Not even the trailing hem of the robe left marks of its passage. It seemed to glide just above the surface of the snow, and I wondered if it had any true "body" in any sense we know.

We were led through the quietly falling snowflakes to a spot where rock thrust up, making a sizable cliff, against which one of the Orhans leaned its venerable boughs. Below the spot where limb met stone, a tall opening loomed darkly. Stooping slightly, Enderon entered, and we followed still, with the Beast at our heels.

Within was a short passageway that seemed a natural tunnel, unshaped and unused by thinking beings. Beyond the second angle of its way, we entered a large chamber that was lit with greenish-golden light, whose source lay at the depths of a pool in the center of the place.

The room itself was smooth and regular as if, in some ancient time, the molten rock of the planet had breathed a bubble of space into this spot, making a lair for Enderon's use.

The pool was a thing of breath-stopping beauty. Its translucent waters quivered with tiny ripples. They were green as new leaves, and through them the golden beams danced, making the shimmering interplay quiver over the glassy walls. I stopped, as we entered, gazing about in delight.

Enderon's gruff chuckle brought me to myself. "There are those who gaze into my chamber and find terror here. I have often wondered what horrors they bear in their souls that are reflected back to them from these polished walls. There are a very few who look with the joy of children, as I do, upon the wonder of it. That you are such folk is a thing that bodes well for our venture. Come sit, and we will talk."

I shook myself and turned to find my two companions doing the same. We moved out onto the floor, which seemed made of black glass. We looked down and saw ourselves looking back up at us, pale faces small above bulky and fur-clad forms. The shape of Enderon, going before us, was not mirrored at all.

I looked back to see what shape the Beast would make, upside-down in reflection. Her white paws, with their neat gray fringes, were set daintily on the floor . . . and where they met the black stone, the shapes of small human feet met them. All above those slender feet was mist. Looking up, I met her eyes, and their sad darkness spoke of things not to be held in words.

When we reached the edge of the glowing pool, we found that it was surrounded by a low lip of stone that flowed up from the floor as a blossom flows from its stem, forming Enderon's couch. We set our packs gratefully upon the floor and settled onto the stone beside our host. Warmth, as well as light, flowed upward from the pool, and we shed our cloaks and outer tunics with their attached mittens, letting them fall about our feet.

The Beast settled herself onto them, very catlike in her aptitude for finding comfort, and looked up at us as if to say, "Let us begin!"

Enderon held up one hand. As the long sleeve fell away, I

could see that the hand was almost as long as my forearm, with seven slender fingers that seemed to have more joints than my own did. Matching the face, the hand was finely wrinkled. There was a sense of terrible strength in it, for all its aged look. One finger went up.

"Firstly," Enderon intoned, "I must warn you that my seeing is not like that of human seers. It is seeing from presence, not distantly from an absent body. Though your physical selves will remain here, you will feel as if they were there with you. If a spear is hurled at you, you will want to drop to avoid it. You must remember that you are not tangible there, however much you may feel your nose itch or your leg cramp with standing. Sudden distraction and motion will rip my concentration and send me back to my own body. In that disruption, it is possible that you might be left behind . . . or sent elsewhere. So remember to remain calm, whatever happens.

Another finger rose beside the first. "Secondly, there will be things that we see and hear that will anger you. This I know, for I have never gone among men without having it happen to me. Anger is a thing we cannot allow to enter our hearts more than fleetingly. It, too, will break the web.

"Thirdly, we will see pain. It is always so in the cities of men. I have looked into your hearts, and I see that you, too, feel for your fellows, be they of your own kind or other. Yet we cannot allow their pain to enter us, for that, too, will destroy my concentration."

It dropped the hand, and the black sleeve again covered that strange member. Then, rising, the Watcher beckoned to us. Lisaux and I rose and went to lie full-length among the furs.

"You will be safe, thus," Enderon said. "The furs will hold the warmth in your flesh, the fires will augment it, and the Beast will watch that nothing outward comes near."

We settled tiredly in the comfort of the pallet, our bones

and muscles melting into the softness. Our eyes grew heavy as we looked up at the figure of Enderon, which now seemed to tower upward to incredible height. Again, it stretched out the arms toward us. The compulsion rose in me, and I moved toward the Watcher . . . but this time I left my flesh behind.

# 16

## *Who See Without Eyes and Hear Without Ears*

THERE was a trembling of the air about me. The green-gold light winked out, to be replaced by a mistiness that seemed to be rushing by with terrible velocity. I felt chill air flowing past my ears. My fingers went numb. It was truly strange, for I knew that both ears and fingers lay snug beneath the furs, watched over by the Beast.

Then I became aware of Lisaux beside me. His shoulder moved against mine now and again, as if we were enfolded in the watcher's consciousness. I could see nothing below or above. It was as if we moved through another dimension between points in our own world. When we slowed, at last, the mist thinned and a white light surrounded us.

We stood—or seemed to stand—on the top of a low wall that overlooked the central circle of the Citadel's inner keep. Behind us, the smokes of the outer city rose, hidden from us by the concentric walls that had made this old city stick in the throats of more than one would-be invader. We looked down into the garden that held in its midst the marble dome in which the High King held court. Strange though it seemed to us, lately beset by snows, here in the southern lands in the shelter of the walls and curving banks of winter-leaved shrubbery, it was almost springlike.

The High King sat upon a bench beside a fountain whose modest spout played in the unfrozen air. Small dark birds picked among the colored pebbles that covered the walk about the bench and the fountain. Now and again one would hop onto the foot of the King and cock its tiny head as if to survey its exalted perch. The King, however, noticed neither birds nor fountain.

He sat immobile, hands on knees, back slightly touching the carven back of his bench. After watching him for what seemed a long time, I realized what it was about him that sent my blood trickling chill through my veins. His eyes were fixed. They did not blink, as a living man's eyes must do. His chest rose and fell by such slow and slight degrees that it was possible to believe that he was not breathing at all.

I turned to Lisaux, who nodded answer to my unspoken question. I turned to Enderon, then, to see if that being had noticed. That tall figure stood on the wall beside me, and its eyes were set broodingly on the figure of the High King.

"Does he live?" I asked softly.

Enderon started, then turned those black and sparkling eyes upon me. "Oh, he lives . . . after a fashion . . . but not as the man I have observed in years past. Something has altered him, removed some vital part of him, leaving a body that waits until some master calls for it. Or so I guess." Enderon fell silent; then in one instant we were no longer on the wall but standing beside the fountain with our feet planted among the small birds, which noticed us not at all.

Now we could look closely into the face of the King. There was no one there. His pale eyes were empty windows, letting no self peer out into the world. He was, in a way, more frightening than any corpse might have been, for the dead are a natural part of the world. This non-dead yet unliving body was alien to everything I had ever imagined.

"Antibius!" said Enderon, quietly but with emphasis. "Antibius, my friend, awake!"

But the King made no motion, no sign that he had heard.

A saucy bird, emboldened by the quiet of the King, flew up and perched on the peaked velvet cap that sat atop the King's dark brown curls. With the most innocent audacity, he relieved himself onto the royal shoulder, leaving a dark splodge on the smooth fur. Without thinking, I leaned forward to brush it away . . . only to find that the fingers that seemed so true and solid to me sank through both cloak and King without affecting either.

Now Enderon's voice brought me to attention. "Watch!"

Three men and a woman moved toward us from an arched door in the dome that centered the garden. Two of the men were richly clad, tall, and of arrogant bearing. The woman was dressed simply in the garb of a Singer who is not on the road: a dark blue robe with the *Huym* worked in silver at hem and wrists.

The third was tall, also. Too thin. Dressed in gray that seemed a continuation of his gray skin. I needed no look at his face and those terrible un-eyes to know that another Ethran drew near. I reached my left hand and touched Enderon. Strangely, there was the feel of solidity in that bony arm, and it comforted me.

"Have no fear," the being said: "they can neither see nor hear us. Even the Ethran cannot, for here he has none of his instruments to scan the world about. The Singer might have known us nearby, but look closely at her."

Wrenching my eyes from the alien, I looked at the woman. It was Ahlia. The clean oval of her face, the incredible violet of her eyes proclaimed it. Yet there was nothing behind that beautiful façade. Even the forbidding expression it had worn when it peered through the oval of gray, seeking the one who called, would have been preferable to the terrible lack that sat there now.

Then I noticed a thing that I should have seen instantly, but for my distraction concerning the Ethran. All three of the human kind moved in a stiff and ungraceful way. They walked as do marionettes in the hands of an unskilled puppeteer. I had no need to question Enderon. The reason for it was obvious.

As the three humans and the Ethran stopped beside the King, the Ethran moved his hand and said, "Antibius, you are wanted. Rise and follow."

At once, the King removed his hands from his knees. Jerkily, one segment at a time, exactly as would a puppet, he rose to his feet and stood at attention until the others walked on. Then he fell in behind the Singer and stalked away, following the Ethran.

Enderon said, "I see. Oh, I do see. May the gods forgive me, their inattentive servant, for I have been remiss. Yet they sent you to me, so they must still have some regard for me, who ill deserves it." The black eyes were clouded with grief as they watched the four out of sight.

Again, without warning, we were elsewhere. This time we stood in one of the wide streets of the city outside the inner keep. Though I had been told many times of the beauty and cleanliness of the Citadel, the orderly and attractive shops and inns, I could see little trace that this had ever been true. Outside the meatmongers shop across the way, a pile of offal gave hint of what its stench would have been, in summer. Slops ran in the gutters, which were stopped and foul with human and animal wastes and vegetable debris.

It was evening, by now, and darkness was creeping up the sky. Lamps and torches were set outside many doors in order to light the streets, and we wandered about, watching, as the dayfolk left their labors and went to their hearths. Even among them, we now and again detected the awkward gait of one whom the Ethran controlled, but their fellows took no notice.

When the people of the night began to move about the streets, we understood much of the reason for the shoddiness of the city. They prowled like preying beasts, and we saw murder and robbery and far worse things in the space of a single street. Not one honest face moved in the city by night. Many of those who so befouled the place were puppets.

"How can he control so many?" I asked aloud.

To my surprise, Lisaux answered. "I hung in the Ethran's web for days and weeks of nothingness. Yet there was something at the heart of that nothingness, for I remember things that I have never known. It may be that in his contempt for our kind, that other Ethran let much of his thought flow through the web of life that held me fast. I know that one of his kind has no need to set his mind to maneuver those who are within his grasp. They have devices, those gray ones, that do their wills with unerring constancy.

"He who now rules Tyrnos holds those at the peak of power within his own mind's orbit. There is no need for his attention to be set upon those who crawl here in the streets. What would you wager, Singer, that each of these bears within his filthy garb a medallion?"

I saw that it must be so. It was galling to think that my kind could be enslaved by symbols and mechanisms, but I swallowed my anger and observed with total attention. If we must come here, we must learn, now, what we could. And in those dreadful streets invisibility was a precious gift. Anything less might well have meant death.

The Citadel, as I had been carefully taught, lies in a series of independently walled areas that have as their common center the keep that we had first seen. There the King and his intimates have their tall houses. There the Council of Commons meets, in time of emergency. There have been times in the history of Tyrnos when all the city has fallen to enemies, save only that inner heart, which is defended by things other than blades and bows.

As one moves outward, the circles diminish in splendor. Those three or four nearest the outermost wall are squalid and crudely built. Yet in this terrible time, the whole of the city seemed soiled and sick. Even the graceful buildings of the inner ways were degraded by a feeling of unhealth, not to mention the condition of streets and doorsteps.

Sickened as we were, we trudged round and round, making the circuit of each alley and avenue that Enderon indicated might be useful to us in the future. Our feet grew sore and blistered, and no amount of inner assurance that my actual feet lay far to the north could persuade those spirit-feet not to hurt me. Lisaux, too, limped, so I knew he felt it also.

We watched the play of the Ethran's tools as they slithered through the dimly lighted ways. When I stumbled upon a newly killed whore who lay in a puddle of her own blood, I stopped in my tracks and closed my eyes.

"Can two alone hope to cure such ills as we see here?" I asked.

Enderon's voice was dry as husks, answering, "No, if you were merely two, alone and unaided. But, silly child, have you not seen and spoken with the kindred of the gods? Have you not been led where you needed to go and given the strength to do the proper things at need? Are you not, even now, standing bodiless in the presence of a myth? Come, now. The gods have you in hand, however helpless you may feel."

I opened my eyes again. Lisaux's haggard face told me that he, too, had known a time of doubt. But Enderon relentlessly urged us onward, and we moved through the night, learning the ways and the houses and the night-folk of the Citadel.

# 17

## Anger Makes a Crimson Light

WHEN we woke into our physical selves in Enderon's bubble, I lay for a short time gazing upward into the mirrorlike dome. The ripple of gold-green light never ceased and never repeated a pattern. The effect was dreamlike and peaceful. It helped to wash away from my spirit the sickness that the ruined Citadel had placed there. Almost, it sent me into sleep.

That was not the plan of Enderon, however. As I followed the ceaseless patternings, the color began, most subtly, to change. A tint of orange came into the gold. The green tinged slowly toward purple.

I sat upright and found the patient Beast looking upward, too. As we watched, the serene glimmerings grew angry and still more angry. Lisaux now sat, and the three of us huddled together as the light from the pool turned from orange to scarlet to deep crimson. The bubble above and about us now resembled an inferno. The crimson light crawled relentlessly about the mirror dome, and it was intermixed with a doomful purple. The place of beauty had become, in the space of a thousand heartbeats, filled with horror.

We turned, as one, to Enderon. It stood beside the pool, and its black eyes stared into the depths. An aura of terrible wrath surrounded the black figure. I knew that the light had changed to match that mood. Even the air had changed; the fresh scent of clean water and stone was charged with an acrid smell.

Enderon looked up, and I saw that I had been mistaken. Not with black eyes but with red ones that being was gazing down at us. Even taller than before, the mythical one loomed over us as though we were children. I found a niggle of fear deep inside myself. Yet there was something reassuring, too. For standing there in wrath, Enderon seemed a match for Ethrans, one or many. What chance had chill gray indifference against such a chaos of bright hatred?

Without speaking, Lisaux and I rose and folded away the fur blankets and set our packs in order again. Though our spirits were worn and weary, the long rest had restored our bodies. We knew that we could afford no time for sleep. Forces had been set in motion; how, I could not quite determine. Perhaps the Gray Sisters had turned their hands to the task. Maybe our bodiless journey with Enderon had upset a delicate balance. Or, more likely, the crimsoning of the pool had awakened powers that had slept for millennia.

Enderon's red gaze was still upon us as we stood before him.

"We will go now, Watcher," I said. Lisaux and the Beast nodded. "You have given us much that we needed to know, for now we understand who our enemy is. There will come after us some . . . perhaps many . . . out of the Sunken Plain. If you will give them aid, it will be of help to all. Watch well, Enderon. It may be that we will need your counseling again."

From deep within, the dry voice whispered, "Go, Children of Riahith. I watch, and now I am awake to my full capacity. Those who follow you will find me waiting for them. If it were my function, I would go in your stead to meet that outworlder who dares to set his will against this world. But I am forbidden. I am the One Who Watches All, and my power is given me for limited purposes. Yet I feel that, should you fail, the gods may remove their restrictions from me. Whatever happens, do not despair. Though you may die, yet Tyrnos will live. That I promise you."

We bowed our heads. When we looked up again, the figure of Enderon was gone. And the light was changing again, growing golden-green, the angry red tint smoothing away.

After the warmth of the cavern, the snowy wood bit deeply into us, even through our furs. To combat the chill, we moved swiftly, the Beast going before as our guide. Unerring as bees in flight we went toward the Citadel; yet three days were required to win free of the wood of Orhan.

Then we stood at the edge of the meadowlands whose stretches were only lightly dotted with snow. Even that was spotted about, leaving broad patches of dead grass and stubble uncovered. At the verge of these lands, the Beast stopped and looked up at us with her sorrowful eyes.

I put my arms about her snowy neck and buried my face in her fur. "We know, Sister. You must go back, now. Yet my heart hurts to leave you, for we have traveled together for many weeks."

Lisaux laid his mittened hand on her back and said, "Go now to the north and westward again, Friend Beast, and find the Holdorn. Bring him and those with him as speedily as may be. The way to the Citadel is now short, and we may need help soon."

She drew herself from my grasp and moved away a step or two. Then she turned and sped away over the snow beneath the Orhans and was soon out of our sight. On an odd impulse, I stooped to look at the pawprints beside my feet. Among them were interspersed, so mingled and mixed as to be all but indecipherable, the prints of small human feet.

With a sigh, I straightened my back and set my face again southward. The mystery of the Winter Beast might well be one that I could never solve.

Now we went even faster, for the lack of snow made the walking easy. It was still cold, though not so much as in the northern places from which we had come. The soil was frozen enough to stabilize the mud of the tilled fields that we now began to cross. We saw houses in the distance, small huddles of farmers' cottages that had been set in squares and circles for mutual comfort and protection.

We avoided them and skirted the broad expanses that might have revealed us to any who were about. Our errand seemed to demand anonymity, and we were determined to preserve it, if that could be done.

For the first time since that brilliant morning at Holdorn, the sun was visible. High and pale it looked, even in these southerly lands. That singing I had done in the mang forest had had greater effect than I had foreseen. Yet I felt sure, trudging along beside Lisaux, that in some manner those snows were of benefit to our purposes, else the gods would not have sent them in such quantity.

The sun showed its face for that day, but when dawn came the next morning, it rose behind woolly rolls of cloud that spoke of snowfall. We rose earlier than the sun and were well on our way when first light came upon us. Now our haste was a driving thing, for we knew that the new snow would slow us, and the Citadel was a long day's march away, we reckoned. Few would note or question two worn travelers who took shelter from a coming blizzard.

We stopped only when our over-weary limbs refused to go on. Then we ate and stretched and helped one another rub the cramps from our leg muscles. So when darkness had begun to edge the clouds to the east, we saw the lumpy mass that was the city lying before us across a wide stretch of farmstead and orchard.

A broad road ran straight toward the city from due east, and we angled to intersect its path. This was the Wayroad that connected the Citadel with Sarnos to the west and Lilion, the border city that hung like a crow's nest in the mountains, to the east. Those traveling across Tyrnos from east to west or north to south were likely to take the Wayroad, for east of the Citadel a half-day's travel it branched north toward Malchion and south to the port city of Langlorn on the southern sea. Unless policies toward travelers had tightened as much as the morality of the city had loosened, none would question the presence of those who entered by the Wayroad. We arrived at the eastern gate amid a bustle of drovers who were bringing the weekly herd to the city for slaughter. As we slipped through the iron-plated portal, the first of the snow spattered against our faces. Then we stood aside from the street, taking shelter in the doorway of a leather shop that had closed for the night.

I might have claimed roof and bed in the School for Singers, with Lisaux as guest. Yet I felt it unwise to let any know that a Singer had entered the city unsummoned. Lisaux, too, felt that we must conceal our names and purposes as long as it was possible, so we agreed to appear as espoused companions and to seek out an inn.

It was no easy task to find one that seemed even moderately clean and well-ordered. Most had degenerated into gathering places for ruffians and worse. Still, we persisted, knowing that when full darkness settled in, we must be off those dreadful streets. At last we found a place nearby the wall of the innermost keep. It had no slops about its doorstep and no carousers in its common room.

As we went up its chipped stone steps, I stopped and clutched Lisaux's arm. Swinging in the snow-laden wind was a sign, as all inns have, painted with its name and symbol. From it stared down the white-furred face and neat dark-rimmed ears of the Winter Beast. Dark, sad eyes and all, it was a likeness that startled us both.

Feeling somehow comforted, as if at a good omen, we entered the place and spoke to the thin woman who sat behind a table watching her customers.

"What manner of beast is it that you have upon your sign-board?" I asked.

Her pinched face brightened a bit, as if some favorite subject had been broached. "Well might you ask," she said. "Many's the wager been made—and forfeited—among those who come here. Some swear that such a creature lived, in very truth, long ago in the forests of Tyrnos. Others scoff, saying that it is mere myth and never lived at all. My own great-grandsire painted that board, drawing from life the beast it shows. He saw it in his youth, in Orhan.

"Let the scoffers say what they will. My grandsire was a truthful man, one not given to careless talk. If he saw it, it exists, or did exist, in Tyrnos. He never gave it a name or a pedigree, but he did say that it lived where the snow lies deep in winter and never came into our southern lands at all."

"Most interesting," said Lisaux. "We have traveled far, my wife and I, and tales such as this delight us. May your stew kettle and your mattress give us as much pleasure!"

This set things off on a cordial footing. She bustled about, cuffing potboys and scolding serving girls, until we were seated and fed. Then we beckoned her to join us in mulled wine against the growing chill of the evening. Her thin nose grew warmly pink as we talked and drank.

"Where be you bound?" she asked us, as the plates were cleared away, and we leaned our elbows on the scuffed board in contentment.

Lisaux looked at me, and I smiled. "We are away to Sarnos, though it is late in the season to make that journey. Yet kinfolk call, and we are bound to answer their need. This snow-fall, if it grows worse, may keep us here for a time. Tell of your Citadel, Lady."

The address pleased her immensely, and she hastened to inform us of the history of the city from the time of the first Ahlia and Radimond, the first of the High Kings.

"It seems a stout city, well-defended and gracefully built," observed Lisaux, when she had paused for breath. "Still, if you will pardon my saying it, it seems a bit down-at-heel, and it does have a certain . . . air."

I buried my unexpected giggle in my winecup. The dame, however, looked troubled.

"Now that, sir, is a very well-taken observation. In my father's time—aye, and when my man was alive and we ran the White Beast together—things were better ordered. The High King was about in the city, looking to grievances and things that needed putting right. His Singer stood one day each week in the Singing-place in the inner keep, and any who were troubled past the knowledge of healers and counselors might go there and have the soul put right. The streets were clean—and safe.

"Yet it is a hard thing to put the right word to, the slipping away of the city from its prime. Mayhap it is just that the High King has grown older, or ill. Ahlia, I know for certain, having seen her recently with my own eyes, looks like the walking dead, so pale and lifeless and stiff she is, nowadays.

"Still, it is a puzzle, and no mistake." She sighed and shook her head.

Not wishing to seem too eager for such information, Lisaux touched my arm and said, "I see that you are weary S-Silira. We must ask this kind dame for our quarters, now, else you will be dozing away."

I yawned obligingly and nodded, as if half-asleep already.

We were led up two sets of angled stairs to a small chamber that opened onto a court at the back of the inn. A blaze warmed the hearth, though I suspected that guests less civil than we did without such comforts. There was a clink of coins, as Lisaux bade our hostess good night at the door. I was already piling my burden of pack and cloak into a corner and making ready to lay me down upon the immense canopied bed that left little room for movement in the small chamber.

By the time my now-worn and dusty russet boots were set aside, and my hands and feet were cleaned in water from the ewer, Lisaux had also relieved himself of his gear. We sank into the oceanlike mattress as if into sleep itself, and the warm comfort soothed us dreamlessly.

We had spun every nerve thin as spiders' webbing. We had strained every muscle many times over. Caution and haste had been our watchwords for too long. Now, in a house watched over by the likeness of the Beast, we lost all sense of danger and let our weariness take us where it would. Only sleep lay in that direction.

# 18

## *Two Harmless Travelers*

WE woke to a timid tap on our door. The white-gray light of a snowy day filled our narrow window, and the room was so cold that our breath smoked mistily. I slipped from the comfort of the downy coverlet and dashed in socked feet to unlatch the door. Then I dived back into bed.

A grubby boy appeared on the threshold. He bore a basket of kindlewood, and he quickly proceeded to lay a neat pattern of the pitchy stuff in the cold hearth, topping it with a cairn of small logs from a box beside the hearth. When he had a goodly blaze crackling, Lisaux pitched him a coin, and he left with a well-pleased smile on his face.

As we waited in unaccustomed luxury for the room to warm, we talked, very quietly. Even an inn guarded by the sign of the Winter Beast might well have ears in its walls, we felt. We knew that Ahlia, and through her the Ethran, knew that some power was awake in Tyrnos. So we spoke as a long-wedded pair might do, of family things and of plans, should we be snowbound in the Citadel.

"I do worry about Mayanna," I said to Lisaux. "And also Leeana and the other children left at home. They might try to follow us, you know, and the way is so long and now covered with snow."

"Do you forget," he said, "that they have good old Rover to find them the way? You might lose men, not to mention children, in the road we have come, but Rover will follow, though we go to the world's end."

I sighed, for it was true. The Beast would find those who came behind us, and she would bring them to us unerringly.

"You are right," I said to Lisaux. "Now what shall we do if we must keep to this city for days, as the snow may force us to do? It is a fine opportunity to see, for once in our lives, a really large and important place. May we ask the dame belowstairs for directions to the palaces and places of interest?"

He chuckled indulgently, and I found time to think how well he played the role into which he had been thrust.

"Of course we may. If we are delayed, it will not speed us at all to sit here in our room and brood. We will walk about and see what is to be seen here. You will have less time to trouble yourself over the . . . problems that your mother faces. Then we will go on, refreshed and enlightened, to help that lady find peace and contentment again."

I thought of Ahlia's blank, dead face, its beauty of line and coloring lost for lack of a spirit to animate it. "Truly," I answered, "we must hurry, when we are able. The Mother of our family is in need of us." The sadness in my voice owed nothing to the actor's art.

A rustle . . . almost inaudible . . . within the wall at the head of the bed told us that our efforts had not been wasted. I felt that all inns and lodging places were probably watched and new tenants spied upon until they were judged harmless. The Ethran, if he resembled his departed kinsman to the north, was no fool in small things. We made no sign that we had heard anything amiss, but proceeded to rise and wash by turns in the crockery bowl that the room afforded.

When we were clean and clad in our lighter furs, we left the room in search of breakfast. As we descended the steep stair, we met other guests on the same errand. We nodded courteously to them and made the salutation that Lisaux had brought with him from Malchion. This labeled us at once as foreign, so that any oddities they observed in us might be laid at that door.

They were unsurprised at finding outlanders among them, for as I said before, the Citadel is at the crossroads of the continent, and those from lands more distant than Malchion pass through its gates. We went down together, two drovers, a hunter and huntress out of eastern Orhan, an elderly dealer in antiquities from Langlorn, and we two harmless travelers.

Our choice of the inn must have been guided by the gods; the table in the common room had been drawn out to its full length and was laden with steaming dishes and etched glass bowls of red and yellow and purple jams and jellies. Hot breads were piled at intervals down the middle, alternating with plates of thin-sliced meat, bowls of steaming porridge, pitchers of creamy milk, and mountains of fluffy eggs.

We stoked our furnaces, Lisaux and I, with more pleasure than had been the case in many long days. Then we took the opportunity to ask the table at large for suggestions as to the best things to see and to do in the city.

One of the drovers piped up, "Jerrim's House of Delights is a proper fine place to go," but the other shushed him.

"Kinna ye see they'm be respectable folk, Derre?" he asked. "What might they be doing at a place like Jerrim's? No, they'm be needing places of interest like . . . like the Cavern of the Kings. That be a spot most travelers do be finding."

"Now for once there's some sense come out of at least one of you two," our hostess said. "Karm's word is a good one, and one I might not have thought on, left to myself. Though it be solemn, in truth, and no place for levity, there is much there that is beautiful and curious and old beyond anything else in the city. I will hunt out my map of the Citadel, so that you may find it without overmuch wandering about. In this weather, to be outside is no pleasure."

So it was that we went away from the Sign of the White Beast that morning equipped with a map upon which were marked not only the Cavern of the Kings but several other places of interest. Among them were the inner keep and the Master Singing-Place in all of Tyrnos.

Snow still fell, but the warmth from many chimneys melted much of it before it could drift the streets deeply. A guard we questioned in the street outside the inn affirmed that, though the inside of the city was well enough, there could be no traveling the Wayroad, for it was drifted chin-deep in places. The gates would not be opened until the road cleared a bit, he said, though messengers and such could come and go through the sally-ports.

Walking was slippery and messy, through slush and muck, but we found our way easily, with the aid of the map, to a knee of stone that seemed to be thrust up into the city from deep below. Cut into the rock was the symbol for Ancient and that for King. The rear part of that outcrop formed a part of the wall of the inner keep. Where the two formed an angle there was a small but ornate gateway crossed with an iron grille.

Though there was no attendant within the narrow tunnel that bored into the stone, a slotted box hinted that offerings would be welcomed. We dropped a pair of coins into it and followed the twisting way deep into the odd formation. There were torches laid ready in piles, all along the way, and we armed ourselves with several and went onward in their flickering light, leaving behind the lamplit entryway.

We found soon that we were bearing downward very sharply, and from the conformation of the land above, we felt that we must be now beneath the inner keep. At a sharp bending of the way, the tunnel opened out into a wide arch, and a stairway cut from the rock itself led away downward, curving out of sight in such a manner to suggest that it spiraled into the deeps beneath this spot.

We were, by now, caught up in the strange aura of the place. Not just to follow our roles as curious travelers did we go down that eery stair. There was a sense within both of us that our way lay through these tunnels, through the Cavern of the Kings, whatever that might be, before it wound upward again into the snowy day. Almost, I could feel Enderon at my elbow, and I wondered if that weird being might not even now be overseeing our activities.

There was a soft chuckle beside me . . . or was it a drip of water splashing from a ledge into a worn cup of rock? Lisaux looked at me sharply, his face all bone, seemingly, in the light of the high-held torch.

"I thought I heard . . ." he began, before letting his voice trail into silence.

"Enderon," I finished for him. "I thought of it, just now, and then it seemed that I heard it laugh beside me. We are not alone, I think."

Now we came to the end of the stair. As we moved from its foot, straining to see the limits of the immense cavern in which we found ourselves, light bloomed from the rock of the walls, dimming our torches to uselessness. We quenched them in a stone cauldron of sand that seemed set there for the purpose and looked about with all the awe of true curiosity seekers.

The cavern arched above, its upper limits lost in shadow, and it curved widely on either hand. Its walls, glistening with mineral and crystalline formations that dripped with slow moisture, moved away from us in such a grand sweep that their further reaches were dim glimmers in the distant deeps. But the walls, splendid as they were, were not the cavern's most spectacular feature.

Out in the center of the chamber stood slender pinnacles of ice whose opposite counterparts could be seen glistening high above, suspended from the distant roof. The cleanliest of sand floored the place, and though it was evident that many came here, it was marked with no track, only slight and regular riffles, as though a steady breeze kept it ever swept clear.

We walked out onto that pristine surface with the same hesitation one feels at spoiling new-fallen snow; but our prints were erased behind us. Then we forgot the sand, the walls, even the esoteric source of the light. Within the first of the ice-pinnacles lay a king.

We were taught, at our School, of the formation of our world, the infinitely slow and meticulous processes that alternated with tumultuous and volcanic upheavals. I well knew that those towers of ice had been patiently a-building long before my kind had been a presence upon our patient planet. Yet there lay that king, his face as peaceful as death had left it, his robe, stiff with gold and gems, undisturbed, his simple circlet of crown upon his head. The ice about him was as clear and unblemished as the finest glass. Surely, this was a mystery within a mystery, not to say a paradox of the purest sort.

We went forward, now, peering anxiously into each of the icy formations. Inside each was a king or a queen. This startled me, for in none of the history that I had been taught was there mention of a reigning queen. Always there had been a king, balanced by a female Singer. Yet, at some time in the distant past, the pattern must have been more flexible. For all these who lay here had been regnants: the symbol *Lyin,* Ruler, was worked into their garments and set in jewels in the simple hoops of their crowns.

We reached the center of the chamber, at last. We would not have known that we were there, except for the manner in which all the ice towers were set. From that point, they moved away like the spokes of a giant wheel, though their arrangement had seemed random from other places. Lisaux looked upward and gave a low exclamation.

He pointed, and I turned my own eyes upward. Infinitely far, at the apex of a cone of suspended stalactites of ice, was a star-shaped light that we recognized must be the day we had left behind. At this spot, with the golden glow of the walls quenched, there must exist one star of light through every day of the world. At the thought, my neck hair twitched, and a shudder of . . . not foreboding, not awe, something more strange and less definable . . . ran through me.

As I thought the thought, the light dimmed from the walls and went to nothing. Then we stood, lost and afraid, in a tiny spot of light whose twilit edges extended less than an arm's length in any direction. Unable to see anything else, we looked down at the sand about our feet. Each grain seemed to sparkle with a separate, silvery glint.

As we watched, those glints fused, became a glow of chill light that became, bit by bit, transparent. We seemed to look down through the sand as if through clear water. At the bottom of the pool lay a key.

Our hands reached downward, simultaneously. Lisaux's arm was longer, the necessary inches I lacked, and his was the hand that brought up that bit of metal through the sand as effortlessly as if it had been, in truth, water. It glowed in his palm with a silver fire, but it was cool when he laid it in mine. At its touch, a thrill of strange energy went from my hand to my head and my heels.

As if kindled by that rush of power, the walls glowed again, more brightly than before. There was something . . . triumphant . . . about the tint of the light that wrapped us round. Carefully, I hid the key away in my pouch. With its swaddling, the light changed to its former hue.

We went away to the foot of that great stair, and I turned back to face the chamber where the Kings and Queens of Tyrnos slept their long sleep.

"Sleep well, longfathers. If the gods will it, we two will set your kingdom to rest again, secure in the hands of your long-distant kin. Yet if that may not be done, we will do our best to right it, however we can, always trusting in the gods to guide us truly. Your gift, it may be, will be the veritable key to victory for us all." So I spoke, as the walls dimmed with infinite leisureliness, and Lisaux again kindled the torches.

The way was long, going up the stair, through the winding tunnels. Four torches' burning saw us to the entryway, and we reckoned that the day must be drawing in, for one torch would burn for over a half-hour. We had no way of knowing how long we had been in the Cavern of the Kings, but that it was long, our thirst and hunger told us.

The gray day told us little, when we emerged from the stony mouth of the place into the deserted cul-de-sac that surrounded it. Still, there was daylight left, and being so near, we wished to see into the inner keep. Again we found our way around the stone formation to the point at which it joined the wall. The grilled gate was locked with a strong metal bar that had in its face—a keyhole! Though I felt that the key in my possession must be a thing more potent than a mere unlocker of gates, I dug it out and tried it in the hole. There was a deep click, and the lock turned.

We looked at one another. Then we shook our heads. We were weary to the bone, all but weak with hunger. Tomorrow must see the next step of our journey completed.

We turned our steps back to the inn, and we were most happy to see evidence of a large and early supper steaming and bubbling and sending out savory smells from the kitchen. Our landlady greeted us with warm interest, and we marveled satisfactorily at the splendor of the ancient tomb of the Kings.

"We spent the entire day in seeing it," I told her. "Does any now living know how the ice was opened for the Kings to be set inside?"

Lisaux added, "We spent much of our time there in wondering how it might have been done, knowing the aeons that cave ice requires to form such height and thickness."

She shook her head, her blue cap waggling unsteadily. "It is an art that has been lost," she said. "Not since the days of our most remote fathers has any king been placed there, for no one knows the way. It seems a pity that our kings must now be laid in tombs of cut stone and earth, when their ancient fathers lie in such majesty. Still, the gods know best, I'll warrant. King or commoner, none of us lie easily, nowadays, either alive or dead.

"But come. I hear the clapper. You must be a-famished, with climbing all those long stairs. We shall test the drovers' meat, this night, and if it be not tender, we'll make them squirm for it."

# 19

## *Keys*

AGAIN we woke to the tap of the fireboy. A grimmer day even than the one before lay outside our window, and we spoke not at all as we lay waiting for the room to warm. It might have been safe to lay bare our entire plan, for there was no faintest sound behind the wall, but we now had nothing to say. Each of us knew that our way was no longer within our own complete control. We suspected that the cleverest plan, the most daring scheme we might devise might well bring us to grief. Now was the time for us to go blindly, trusting the scheme of the gods that was unwinding about us. It was a helpless feeling. We were both bold and determined folk, and our native instincts were frustrated by this necessity for walking an unseen maze, totally dependent upon other wills than our own.

We dressed with only slight and friendly comments and went into the hall. A stranger was moving from our door toward the stair, and we gave him good morning, as we all went down together.

He looked as if our greeting startled him, but he jerked out a civil reply, and we sat down together when we reached the common room. This meal matched that of the morning before, and we were too busy for a time to make conversation.

Our two drovers had gone, braving the snow through the sally-port to return to their homes across the farmland to the east. The hunters were there, but they had little to say and seemed uncomfortable at being between walls for so long.

The elderly antiquarian was in full cry, exclaiming over the artifacts he had found in the shops of the city, as well as those he hoped to purchase from families that had known better times. After a long soliloquy concerning a jeweled cup that he had found amid the rejected things in a shop dealing in used items of the commoner sort, he turned to Lisaux.

"How did you find those caverns they told you about? Worth the walk, were they? Much there—my sort of thing?"

Lisaux smiled. "We found the Cavern of the Kings most interesting. We spent the day there, almost, but I cannot say that there was anything there that you might have bartered for. It is unguarded, which tells you much about its contents. Except for the kings themselves, frozen deep in ice, and the sand of the floor and the stone of the walls, there is nothing. It is well worth the trip, if you are intrigued by history."

I smiled brightly at the man and said, "You really *should* go. The walk is long, true, and the tunnels and stairs quite exhausting, but you will find it fascinating."

I knew that if we had discouraged him from the trip, he would have suspected that treasures lay about for the taking. I could envision him chipping madly away at the encasing ice, his jowls quivering with effort, after the gemmed robes and crowns of the kings and queens who slept there. And, while I suspected that there were safeguards there that the eye could not see, I hated the thought of his money-hungry eyes devouring that place.

He lost interest at once, as we had known he would. The lack of guards, if nothing else, persuaded him that there was nothing there worth the taking.

Now the conversation became more general. Our hostess

began listing all the places in the Citadel where one might find old and valuable things for sale. We pretended interest and took part in the talk, but I caught the eye of the new member of our group, more than once, when I glanced toward him. He was studying, very discreetly, the both of us. The suspicion that he had not been just passing by our door grew in me, as we sat there.

Taking the bold course, I asked him, "And what is your business here in the Citadel amid the snow? I feel that all of us, just now, are caught here unexpectedly by the storm. Are you fretting over troubled kin, as we are, or are you neglecting business at Sarnos or Lilion?"

His eyes, for once, did not shift away from mine. With a start, I knew that this was another who carried the degraded *Huym*. The same dullness of expression lay behind his yellowish eyes. Yet I kept my voice steady and my expression bright as I teased, "Come now, tell us your secrets!"

His smile was a travesty, but he managed it. He mumbled something about business in the west at Sarnos and sank into silence again.

I looked across the table at Lisaux and saw that he had missed nothing. He nodded slightly, and I rose and stretched.

"We might cheerfully sit here and while away the day with stories, but our children will want to know everything about the city, from outer gates to inner keep. We had best be about our exploring. It is ill enough to be away from them. At least we can bear home tales of the things we have seen." So speaking, I shrugged on my cloak and took up several rolls that had been left over from our breakfasting.

"We all but starved, yesterday," I said to the dame. "This time I will have something to stay our stomachs, if we become engrossed again."

With much to-do, she insisted on making a lunch for us, laying slices of meat inside the rolls and bringing out a bottle of fruit wine to put with the rest. We laughingly thanked her and laid a generous pourboire beneath a napkin for her to find later.

The street, when we reached it at last, was even more dismal than before. Now a biting wind whipped down the streets, bearing on its back more snow. We bundled our hoods about our ears and thrust our mittened hands into our pockets against the cutting edge of the cold. It was hard, now, to remember summer, the warm dust of the roads, the gentle touch of the breezes. It seemed that I had lived in a winter world for all of my life, with toes and fingers constantly nipped.

We took a roundabout way, this time, toward our destination, for nothing else of interest to travelers lay about the Cavern of the Kings . . . except only that grilled gateway into the inner keep. If there were those who kept an interested eye upon our movements, those movements must be the innocently random ones of true sightseers. So we wandered through shops, admiring delicate laces from the ships at Langlorn, fine leather goods from the Citadel's own craftsmen, and subtle gems from the edges of the world.

Among the last we found a little ring of some silvery metal —not true silver, indeed, but something harder, brighter, less easily identified Indeed, the dealer himself knew nothing of its nature. Set into that ring was a stone of the true greeny-gold that had burned in Enderon's bubble. On its center, a spot half the size of my smallest fingernail, was finely incised the *Huym*. Interlaced with it so intricately that it was difficult to trace the outlines of either was the *Lyin*. The meaning of that web of symbolism took my breath. For what it defined was the Ruling Singer, and only one had ever borne that title. This small and insignificant circle had once belonged to the first Ahlia.

"Another key has been given to us," Lisaux muttered into my ear, and I smiled foolishly, for the shopkeeper was watching us, and exclaimed, "Oh, my dear! It will be too expensive, I know!"

At that, the shopkeeper came forward with his best manner and said, "This small token is no great treasure, to be priced beyond your means, I am sure. A pretty thing, is it not?" He took it from Lisaux's hand and held it to the light. In his wrinkled paw, its silver color dulled, the gem cooled to grayish, as if it had no wish to be recognized by other eyes than ours. With a grimace, the man held it beneath his glass and scrutinized the gem closely. Then he named a figure so reasonable that it made me blink.

"I . . . believe I can spare so much," said Lisaux. "My wife has borne our delay so patiently, she deserves reward."

So the ring was paid for. Refusing the offer to wrap it, I put it upon my finger forthwith. When we walked into the street again, the finger within its circle was warm, and from that warmth spread a fine glow that soon had me unfrozen from ears to heels.

With the warming came a sense of purpose. "We must go now!" I said to Lisaux. "I feel that this is our final key. There is need, now, of haste. My blood drums with it, and my spirit stuggles to free itself and run ahead toward the gate beside the Cavern of the Kings. Whoever watches us now will learn nothing that he has time to use. Come!"

He nodded, and we sped up the snowy street, from which even the guards seemed to have disappeared. Unencumbered with the need for pretense, we found ourselves beside that strange knee of rock far sooner than we had thought. Following its curve, we once again approached the grilled gate.

The key from the Cavern was in my hand as we came up to it, and it was unlocked, passed, and relocked as quickly as it takes to tell of it. The garden within was evidently one little used, even in summer, for shrubbery grew straggly and untended. Grasses had been let to run tall and to dry like standing hay. A graceful marble pergola stood in the center of a pool that was now filled only with snow, and none had troubled to sweep that white carpet from the walks that led from that spot to an unobtrusive door in the wall of the house that turned its back toward the place.

We moved along those snow-covered ways, knowing their path by the decorative stone borders that paralleled their edges. At the steps before that singularly self-effacing door, we paused and looked up at it. Upon its plain panels was carved a small symbol—the interlocked *Huym* and *Lyin*. We had come to Ahlia's very door.

Confidently, I sped up the three shallow steps and set my hand to the iron-wrought latch. It seemed to be welded into position, but I pulled away my mitten and let the ring shine out into the gray day.

The silvery metal gathered light into itself until it shone like a small sun through snow clouds. My finger, indeed my whole hand, tingled with its strange life, and the latch before my eyes changed its color from black to steely gray. It began to hum, as metal sometimes does in a thunderstorm. The pitch grew higher, higher, becoming almost unbearable to the ear. There was a tiny click, and the latch dropped, unaided, letting the door swing silently open.

Lisaux followed me into the chilly hall beyond.

I wondered, looking about me, that each succeeding Ahlia had not made the place her home. Yet it was obvious that many generations of bats and mice and other less inoffensive things had been the only tenants. The tall windows of painted glass were so grimed and obscured that the dim day outside did nothing to light the gloom. We ignited a lightglass and stood looking about us.

The hall ended in tremendously wide, high-arched doors. They stood open, and our light shone into the chamber beyond, its hard white glare glancing oddly from the walls that shaped an octagon. Opposite us gaped another pair of doors, even more magnificent than those we stood by. Between was a broad expanse of marbled floor that seemed littered with millennia of droppings. Disturbed by our light, bats squeaked above us, and we found that the carven ceiling was festooned with tiny black bodies.

Lisaux moved the light about, seeking for the thing, whatever it was, that we had been sent to find. Then he steadied it upon the grand fireplace, one of two that dominated opposite sides of the room. Above it, cut into a slab of gemlike material, appeared again the symbol of the first Ahlia. Drawn, we moved toward it, ignoring the scuttling of small living things through the debris about our feet and the cries of the bats above us.

As our light held the carven slab, it began to glow. I held out the ring, and it added its effulgence to the beam that now illuminated the thing. The symbol began to pulse with silver that turned, by degrees, to the same greenish-gold that lit the stone of the ring. So we stood there, focusing our light and our minds upon the symbol before us.

It throbbed on the wall, seeming almost angry in its pulsations. As it did, there came a note from the stone itself, a deep hum that vibrated in the bones and made the teeth feel loose in my mouth. As it sounded, there came a grating from within the ancient fireplace.

I stooped and drew Lisaux down to shine the light into the sooty opening. The stained marble of the firewall pivoted, protesting at every finger-width, until it stood side-on to us. Beyond it was a tunnel that was darker than the worst fear I had ever known. But it was obvious that this was the thing we had come to find, so we bent double and crept through the cobwebbed way, fending filmy strands away with wild waves of the arms. As soon as we had passed the fireplace, we could stand erect again, and with much disquiet I heard the stone pivot closed behind us.

The lightglass glared whitely upward from Lisaux's hand, making skulls of our faces. We stared for a moment, eye into eye. Much misgiving was in the face of my companion, and it was a match for mine, I do not doubt. We were unfamiliar with the inner keep, save only that part we had seen as disembodied minds in the company of Enderon. We had no idea where the tunnel might lead us, no premonition, even, of what awaited us there. For a span of heartbeats, blind panic hovered close.

Then, most strangely, I seemed to hear the purr of the Winter Beast. Her neat white face came to my mind, the dark eyes looking into mine with their unutterable message. I sighed, and with that slight sound, the spell was broken. Lisaux turned and moved down the tunnel, sweeping the white light before us as if it were some magic broom that might whisk away any peril that lurked there.

The way was not cramped, but it wound dizzily, evidently following the angles of walls and the pitches of stairways. Within ten paces, neither of us could have said in which direction our point of entry lay. We grew less oriented as we went. To add to our unease, we fought our way through dense veilings of webs—webs so large and of such coarse spider silk that even mice and small bats were caught up in them, in every stage of decay. Worse yet, there came from ahead and behind dim chitterings and scritchings that might have had their source in any of the dark myths the grannies used to tell by the fire at night.

Yet, shuddering, I went forward behind Lisaux, thanking the gods for sending me into this task companioned by such a stalwart champion. Alone, I might have entered here. I might even have won through to accomplish the task assigned me. But I would have left my sane balance behind me in these hellish tunnels.

We came, at last, to the end of our wanderings. The passage ran straight for a time, without the side passages and culs-de-sac that had complicated it. It ended against a plain wall that seemed to be made of well-laid stone blocks.

"It opens," I said, my voice booming and muttering away behind us.

"Aye," grunted Lisaux, bending to look closely at every part of the barrier.

The light cast the masonry into a crosshatched sketch of black shadow on white stone . . . and one of those lines was infinitesimally wider than those before and behind it. Lisaux was upon it before I could open my mouth to tell him of it. With his knife blade, he pried delicately at the crack. It seemed solid and immovable.

"Wait," I said, holding out the hand that wore the ring. "This may open yet another way."

It did. The stone glowed in the white light, gold flickers moving through the green aura it cast. The chitterings behind us in the tunnel died away, leaving a sudden silence. The air grew heavy; even the dust we had raised seemed to settle abruptly into old places. My eyes fixed upon the crack in the stone and locked there. No act of will could have drawn them away; I knew that Lisaux's were also focused there.

With a groaning sigh, the solid masonry moved, showering us with dust and grit. It slid aside just enough for one person to sidle through, and its waiting attitude made us hasten, for we knew that it, too, would close behind us.

We found ourselves behind thick curtains or tapestries in a narrow gap that was stifling with old air and older dust. Moving out, we stood in an arched bay. Directly before my questing eye were tiers of marble benches that held cushions of scarlet and gold and ivory velvet. Their empty reaches stretched impossibly far, filling an immense hall whose domed roof arched out of my sight above. There was no sound, no breath of any tenant there. I stepped through the draperies and stood looking at the polished wall that centered the curtained space.

Lisaux, coming behind me, gasped. "Is this . . . ?" he asked.

I nodded. "Yes. We have come into the very soul of the Citadel. This is the Singing-place where Ahlia sang when she was Ahlia. It has been long, I feel, since any voice was raised here to heal the soul of anyone in Tyrnos."

"The Ethran . . ." mused Lisaux. I laughed. We had traveled together for so long that we were like two elderly folk, long wed, who can read thoughts without need of words.

"If there is anything the Ethran fears," I cried, my voice ringing through the shape of the hall, true and clear, without distortion, "it is this place, when a Singer stands here!"

# 20

## The Music of Truth

NOW that I stood in the spot toward which the gods had impelled me, I felt no hesitation. I knew, unerringly, what I must do, as did Lisaux.

I moved toward the Singer's perch, climbing the graceful stair and finding the exact center of the semicircular platform. Behind me, the polished stone of the wall began to glow with soft light. Before me, the hall waited in the chilly snowlight that fell through curved skylights far above. The air waited; the stone waited; the empty benches were tenanted by waiting ghosts. All those dead kings, I felt, were there, with all the many Ahlias.

Lisaux drew the black blade, set the black shield on his arm, and faced outward, guarding the foot of my stair. Any who sought to stop my song would find the task difficult.

Then I forgot what was there, who was there. I closed my eyes and drew a deep breath, then another. The Power, which had always coursed strongly through me at such times, now threatened to lift me bodily from the platform. This would be no common Singing, I had known from the beginning. No single soul waited for healing. And one cannot sing the soul of a country back to health again, however powerful he may be.

I had no inkling what my Singing might accomplish. No intuition told me that the King or Ahlia or any other might thereby be freed from the Ethran's spell. Yet the gods had set me here, after much difficulty and danger. The Gray Sisters turned their attention toward me, I well knew, with death my forfeit for failure. And Enderon, that enigmatic Watcher, still watched, without doubt. If I channeled the Power truly, then all might be well. Still, I did not forget the words of the Gray Ones, as I prepared.

Strange as it may seem, their threat comforted me. Had I felt the possibility that by my own error Tyrnos and the world might be lost to the Ethrans, I could not have loosed one note. Yet I had their promise that I would die before such could happen. Power surged strongly into my throat.

I opened my mouth and sang.

One is born with a voice capable of singing well. Years of training and practice make it an instrument that is flexible and strong. Inspiration can take it to heights of power that it would be incapable of reaching otherwise. But for the first time in all my life, I felt the gods sing directly through me, honing and refining the thing in my throat into something that no human creature could attain without their aid.

As the first note trumpeted through the hall I opened my eyes. Sustained beyond the possibility of breath, that note moved outward through the stone walls. I felt it go out in a ring of flawless sound, wider and wider, lapping the city in its circle.

My throat moved slightly, muting the single note until the diminuendo died to silence.

It stood for ten heartbeats in the midst of that startled silence, and the city without the wall of the inner keep woke with a hum of voices that seemed to shout and to pray. As I waited upon the music, something woke into being, there within the hall. Though it had no shape, no color, no texture, I knew it for the self of the Ethran, roused to fear and anger by the presence of such as I within its most secure place.

Again I breathed deeply. My lungs seemed to have doubled their capacity, and I filled them. Then the music moved forth again, sharp stabs of sound that moved up the scale by half-tones. As they thrust through the hall, I felt the Ethran flinch away from them as if they pierced it painfully. At the topmost note, a long tremolo began, and before it the alien being was helpless. He fled the hall, seeking his sheltering flesh.

As he disappeared from my inner senses, the device through which he had brought himself there shattered into bright shards.

Now the music flowed from me with the irresistible power of a river or a tide. Sometimes sonorous, sometimes light and rippling, it embodied all that had made our land a place where people lived as happily as our kind may ever do. As it rose and fell, I heard crashes and tinklings both within and without the hall. I guessed that the Ethran had set many of his devices to watch and to compel his captives. With great care, the gods were breaking them.

With some inner sense, I knew that the walls of the Sing-ing-place were acting as amplifiers, sending the sound within it outward with augmented intensity. The city was waking to full awareness. I could feel the tensions build as mind after mind snapped to attention and looked about, seeing the grim thing that had been done to the city and its folk.

Held up by some force outside myself, I stood and sang. There came a time when the doors of the hall burst open to admit armed men. They came with the stiff gait that bespoke the carriers of the debased *Huym*, but they were many. Their faces were stamped with death.

Lisaux stepped forward, as I sang a crescendo that stopped them in their tracks by its sheer volume. Then the dark blade was busy, and I could hear, even through my singing, the clang of metal against metal. I closed my eyes, that I might not be distracted by my concern for Lisaux. My loss would be great, my guilt greater, if I must return to Leeana without him, but I thrust the thought from my heart.

The music went on inexorably. The battle below me raged, the stink of blood and entrails finding its way even to my tall perch. Yet, in the grip of the gods, I did not falter. Whatever happened there below, I must go on to the end. Strangely, the dire weariness that had been wont to overcome me while singing did not touch me. It seemed that the voice of the gods moved through my body without touching it. My throat did not dry or become raw; my legs did not waver. I stood as if I were carved from the stone of the platform and let the music flow out.

At last, it began to die away. Three fading repetitions of the final phrase drifted across the hall, each more softly than the last. I opened my eyes as stillness came again, and I looked down.

The hall seemed painted, but the paint was blood. Men lay sprawled in the undignified attitudes of death all about the arc of clear space that separated the platform from the foremost tier of benches. Released from the grip of the gods, I vaulted from the platform, begrudging the time to descend the stair, and hunted through the tumbles of bloody armored flesh, seeking for Lisaux.

I found him soon. His black cuirass made a spot of darkness amid the steely mail of the others. He was half-buried beneath men, some of whom still groaned feebly as I hauled them aside to reach him. He was still alive when I drew him free, straightening his limbs along the floor and laying one of the bright cushions beneath his head.

He was battered and slashed, but I could find no deep, thrusting wound that seemed of a fatal sort. His helm was deeply dented over his left ear, and I thanked the gods for its stout metal. When I had lifted his head and taken away the helm, he drew a sighing breath and opened his eyes.

"Be still!" I said, holding him down with the hand that still wore the ring. "You may be more hurt than I can tell."

Still, he insisted on sitting, and I helped him, when I could not dissuade him. He looked down at the shambles in which we sat, and he groaned and tears came to his eyes.

"I had hoped never to see such things again," he whispered. "Death is not a gift I willingly bestow."

"Sssshh!" I hissed, drawing the wine bottle from beneath my cloak. "You fought for the gods. Never regret it!" And I gave him the wine, which he sipped, then doused upon his more gaping cuts.

"What?" he asked suddenly, trying to rise to his feet. I motioned him to sit again and went to the door to find the cause of the tumult that had suddenly begun outside.

A white shape almost flattened me as it bolted in through the door and began leaping about me, purring with delight and making deep, growly comments. Then a shout rang out, and I gasped with joy.

"Holdorn!" was the cry. The clanging of blade against blade, the sibilant swish of arrows filled the inner keep.

Now the Beast had found Lisaux and was going over him, bit by bit, licking his wounds with great care. He shut his eyes and his jaw tightened, but he made no protest. When she had done, she laid her head against his shoulder as if in apology for the pain she had caused, and he patted her neck.

The battle outside was deafening. I wondered who was still controlled by the Ethran, to fight for him so well. Then I thought of those who bore the *Huym*, and I guessed that there had been many whom the Ethran had subverted, with the aid of Ahlia.

We crouched there in the spattered hall, and the Beast sat beside us as if that outer battle were none of her concern. She sat as if waiting, and her dark eyes looked ever toward the curtained wall that flanked the Singing platform. After a time, I ceased to hear the cries and groans from outside as I, too, listened for something quieter, more subtle . . . more deadly.

It came, as our hearts had told us it would, from behind the draperies. They bellied with motion behind them, as one moved sidewise along that musty space to emerge beside the platform and stand facing us.

Ahlia. Alone, her beauty terrible in its vacancy until, as she stood, a soul came back into the space behind her eyes. But it was no beautiful soul that looked out at us from those violet eyes. Her lip curled with contempt as she turned and began to climb the stair to the Singing-place.

I groaned and began to drag myself upright, finding that my strength had evaporated with the last of the Power. The Beast set her paw upon my shoulder and pushed me down again. Then she stood proudly upright on her four dainty paws and looked up at Ahlia, who now stood in her rightful place of Power.

The Singer inhaled once, twice, and her mouth opened. Her throat strained, the corded muscle and the curve of larynx standing out starkly, but no sound came forth. Her face grew ugly with anger, and she tried harder, forcing a croak from her mouth. The violet eyes went wide with shock, and I thought to myself that she had not tested her art in all the time that she had been in league with the Ethran. She had taken for granted that which is solely a gift of the gods, and they had reclaimed their gift.

I felt pity for her as she sank to her knees on the stone. The polished wall behind her began to glow, and the Beast began to sing.

Once before I had heard that eery song. Here it was stranger, more powerful, more compelling than any music I have ever heard. Its quavers rippled through the hall and were limned on the wall behind Ahlia in sharp lines of black and white. Ahlia's soul began to form there.

A Singer seldom sees a soul sung, save in her own mind. This was an alien thing . . . a soul foreign to any I had ever sung, for even that of the Ethran had been that with which it had been born. This was a soul whose keeper had knowingly distorted it, warped it from the ways the gods have always taught to be true. It was a deliberately wicked thing, yet hollow as the mind that thought to do such an unhallowed thing.

Singing, the Beast began to climb the stair. Singing, she walked out onto the half-moon shape of it and looked down at Ahlia. Singing, she stood erect on her hindmost paws and reached high with her forepaws. Then the ululations of the Beast became a clear human voice. For two heartbeats we stared at the wall behind her, where a clear and flawless human spirit was drawn, washing away the warped thing that had been there.

As the song reached its climax, the shape of the interlocked *Huym* and *Lyin* traced itself in green-gold across the wall.

"Ahlia," I breathed and sank to my knees.

Lisaux, beside me, bowed his head and made his own Holy Sign. We kneeled there, awestricken, as the notes rang to one last triumphant climax that was quenched with shattering mastery, at its height.

The first Ahlia stood on the platform beside her distant daughter. Their faces were similar—would have been the same, except for the difference that shone in their eyes. Ahlia-who-had-been-the-Beast looked down upon Ahlia-who-had-become-less-than-a-beast, and her eyes flashed violet flame.

The recumbent Ahlia raised her head, glaring from eyes that seemed to have lost any humanity they had ever known. Their gazes locked. An almost visible current of violet flowed between them. Stiffly, compelled more truly that she had been even by the Ethran, the second Ahlia stood. Twinned, they glared eye into eye.

"Now there must be a reckoning," said she who had been the Beast. Sweeping her hands wide, she drew them inward in a gathering motion. The two winked out, and the dais was empty.

# 21

## *Ethranen*

AGAIN the hall was still. Those who had moaned now were silent, whether unconscious or dead I could not tell, though I moved among them and tried to determine which of them yet lived.

The battle had died away while the Ahlias had stood together on the Singing-place. There was a stillness wrapped about the city and the keep that might have rivaled that of the dead. Lisaux slept, and I moved softly, that I might not wake him. His breathing was so light that only by the motion of his chest did I know he lived at all. Not a wind whispered, not a beast cried out. The quiet thump of my heart might have been a war drum, so loud did it seem in the stillness.

The battle was not yet done. I knew it and had known since the instant the two had disappeared from the hall. There was yet the Ethran, and this one was forewarned, armed with subtle devices of his race, and angry with the wrath of one deprived of stolen things.

He had not fled from me, that gray one, but from the danger of his devices' shattering, which would have left him bereft of flesh. He, I well knew, had marshalled those who were entrapped in the bitter battle against the Holdorn and his followers. If he had won, mine would now be a terrible

contest. If he had lost . . . an even more bitter fight lay before me. He and his brothers coveted a world. I was the only
thing that they could see standing in their path. Their vision,
fortunately, I knew to be blinded when they looked toward
those who were instruments of the gods.

I looked about the hall, which was now dimming, as the
light died from the gray sky above the skylights.

"Enderon!" I called softly. No answer came, but I might
have felt the smallest of breezes touch my cheek.

"Sisters of the gods!" I called, more loudly. "Are you here?
Do you see? Aid me!" But to that there was no reply of any
kind. I felt the edges of despair lapping at my spirit.

I went to the door and looked out. The keep was littered
with dead things, men and animals. Nothing stirred there.
No sound moved in all the city. I felt as if I were locked into
a bubble of stillness that only one thing might open. Until the
Ethran came forth to do battle, I could only wait.

Weariness settled upon me like a black cloak, I lay on a
bench and put my head upon a gold cushion. With a slow
finger, I traced the *Huym* in the air above me. Then sleep
bore me away.

I woke to complete darkness. Yet the stillness that had been
so all-encompassing had been flawed. Something moved
within the hall. Not Lisaux, for some sense within me knew
that he slept his fevered sleep as yet. Not the Beast. The feel
of her presence was unmistakable. Something stood below
the lip of the platform. Something that gave out a gray aura,
even in blackness.

I sat. Then I stood and walked forward, setting my feet
carefully that I might not be overthrown by one of the corpses
on the floor. There was no hesitation, for I knew as surely as
one could know that my enemy was before me. The ring
began to warm upon my finger.

I raised my hand. The stone was glowing like the eye of a
wild thing in torchlight. Moment by moment, it grew

brighter. I held it high and swept its beam to draw a giant *Huym* across the dark.

The hall began to light itself. By whatever means the Cavern of the Kings was illumined, so also was the hall. The light grew until we stood, the Ethran and I, in a bowl of golden splendor. The ring, strangely, did not dim in that radiance but seemed to glow more brightly still.

The Ethran's dull shape was a stain on the fabric of our world. His narrow form, his non-eyes reflected no part of the light. He moved his hand, and a squarish device within it gave a shrill squeal. As he raised it to point its narrow end at me, I traced another symbol in the air between us. There came a crack of sound, a pulse of purplish light, the stink of something burned. As if to test the thing, he swept it toward one of the dead. The armored figure sizzled and shrank to nothing.

"You, Singer?" he said questioningly. "How have you thwarted the *yehli*? Your folk have no technology; we have learned that unarguably. You cannot thwart the *yehli* without the use of some device!"

"I have nothing to say to you, alien," I answered. "All that I wished to know of your kind I learned from one of your kindred . . . who now wanders, formless, in the spaces he was used to traveling across.

"You, however, have proven that you cannot learn about my kind. Faced with the proofs of our powers, you scoffed, I do not doubt, just as your brother did. Now you must suffer those powers and go into the dark, uncomprehending."

I spoke with rather more confidence than I truly felt, for as yet I did not know how it was that I must do battle with the thing. I was past a Singing, though that had put his kinsman to flight. Unless the ring . . .

As the thought came to me, I slipped the circle from my finger and held it before me. At that moment, a bolt of energy sprang from the shape in the Ethran's hand. The light of the ring absorbed it, and the stone grew even brighter.

The Ethran, however, stood staring at the thing in his hand. "Y'igh? Y'igh? Are you there?" he cried into the box, and I knew that I had faced more than one of his kind, just now.

"Ar'tagh? Speak!" he shouted. But those who had linked with him through the thing were linked no longer. He faced me alone, and his device was a useless shell in his gray hand.

"You will go, with all your kin, from our world," I told him. "They, I'll be bound, are gone before you, for the stone in this ring is purring like a well-fed cat. It has sent them outward, whence you all came. Perhaps justice awaits you there. It is no concern of ours."

I swept the beam from the ring up and down him, back and forth across him, and his gray form faded, faded, and was gone.

The bubble burst. Shouts and cries and callings poured into the hall from outside, and the voice of the Holdorn rose high above all. The door was suddenly full of people, a ragtag lot clad in furs and woollens and shepherds' fleeces. Leeana stood there, and Mayanna.

With the last of my strength, I pointed toward Lisaux. I saw the frail and indomitable woman leap over corpses to reach him. I saw, as if from a distance, Mayanna look at me with alarm, and the Holdorn shoulder aside those who stood between us as he started to my side. Then they all dissolved into the fog that unaccountably filled the chamber and hid the world away.

When I woke, another day was half sped. I lay in a room that seemed cut from topaz, so bright and translucent were its walls. Windows let in a dazzle of snowlight, and I knew that the sun must be shining again. Turning my head, I could see that my leather breeches and jerkin, newly oiled and fresh, lay upon the chair there. In another, Mayanna dozed, her head nodded forward but her back as straight as it had been when she stood in the kitchen at Holdorn while Ruif's men threw things at her.

Quietly, I rose and donned my clothing, finding fresh new smallclothes, which I sadly needed, beneath the leathers. As I washed, my companion woke.

We smiled at one another for a long moment.

"I take it that we won the Citadel back from those who held it?" I asked.

"We fought the hands," she answered, taking my own hand in hers, "and we lopped them off. You and Lisaux scotched the head and sent it—where?"

"Only the gods know that," I replied, following as she opened the door. I peered down the ornate hallway and asked, "Where, by the bye, are we? I am nigh as lost as the Ethran, for I remember nothing since I fell in the hall."

"Come," she said, leading me forth. "We are in the House of the High King. He is waked to himself again, full of pain and shame that he allowed himself to be caught so. Lisaux and Leeana are down the passageway and asked to see you as soon as you woke."

Lisaux lay in a tall bed, looking most ill-at-ease there. Lee-ana sat by his side, and I knew that only her stern will would keep him flat until he was well-healed. But both smiled when we entered the room, and I clasped Lisaux's hand in both my own.

"My brother," I said, "it would have been no victory if you had died. My family is lost to me, for Singers are taken very young and never come to know their kin. You and yours will be my family, now, if you will have it so. And I will walk the roads of Tyrnos, warmed and comforted in the knowledge that in the high places of Malchion I have those who hold me in heart."

"But the High King wishes to see you," said Mayanna. "He wants you to accept Robe and Ring as Soul-Singer of Tyrnos, highest of your order. You need not walk the roads again."

I shook my head. The feel of the leather was good against my skin. I could smell, in memory, the dust of summer puffing before my worn russet boots. The road . . . the road I had chosen, and to the road I would keep.

"I am unfit. Too young, unschooled in courtly things. There is one, the Singer who directs the School where I was trained, who is far more fitted than I for such a task. Ask the High King to send for Elysias to be his Singer. And hint to him that the School in the Citadel might well be closed until those within it may be examined for . . . taint. Perhaps it should be closed entirely. It would be so easy for corruption to touch it, here in the seat of power."

Lisaux nodded, his eyes on mine. "This is your will," he said, and it was not a question. "Well did I know that it would be. I have walked beside you, fought beside you, watched you face forces that chilled my blood. I knew that you could not sit within walls and watch the seasons change.

"But I have lived, also, with kings. They are grateful— after a fashion. They dislike having their gratitude declined. It would be well if you would go now, leaving us to persuade him that you were too young and unassuming to realize that he might wish to reward you.

"Go with the gods, Yeleeve."

My name startled me. How—when had he learned it? But it was the only thing I possessed, and I made a gift of it to these three who were my own. I kissed each warmly, and I left the room and the House and the city itself and walked away down the road.

East—I would go east. . . .

# *Epilogue*

ON the eastward road, I was met by the Winter Beast. When I went to my knees, down in the snow, and did obeisance to her, she licked my face and teased me with her whiskers until I laughed and was her friend again.

Then she danced away across the snowy fields, and I followed her. We went very fast, for she broke trail for me as Lisaux had done. We reached the Orlian quickly, for here it dipped far toward the Wayroad, and once within the wood we fairly flew.

Deep inside the wood, the snow was thin. Many beasts had moved about, tracking the whiteness. As the sun of the third day reddened the tops of the ancient trees, I saw a figure far ahead.

"Enderon!" I cried, as I had done in the Singing-place. This time it answered: a dry chuckle and a hail.

The Watcher waited for me, then leaned down to take my hand. Together, with the Beast dancing about us, we moved through the wood to the arched entryway into the magical gold-green cave. The dark tunnel was now familiar, and I emerged into the light-shot space with joy.

The pool sent its springlike fires upward, and the patterns moved upon the mirrored dome as they had done before. But one thing was different. Some one lay beside the lip of the pool, her blue robe a dissonance of color, the shape of her spirit a dissonance of being. Ahlia, the ivory oval of her face sunken and old, the violet of her eyes still sparking baleful fire.

Now we moved forward over the black-mirror floor, and I saw the Beast's small human feet very clearly. Above them, in the reflection, rose a tall white figure, going away deep into the floor, its pale hair only a glimmer above the white robe hem and arms. The Beast looked back at me, and in its eyes was a serenity that flowed over me like cool water.

We reached the pool, and the Beast nudged Ahlia until she stood.

We looked at one another, the oldest Singer of my order and the youngest. "I would have withered you as you stood, had you dared to come against me!" she spat. "Only the gods could stand against me!"

I looked at her and found pity within me. "Had I come against you, you would not now stand here, I think," I said at last, and stepped back and away from her.

The Beast pushed the woman to the benchlike lip of the pool and butted her until she stepped up on it. Enderon moved behind them, and the three were caught up in the fires that pulsed outward from the green water. Enderon moved long hands, and the waters moved aside, to left and right. I saw that dark green steps descended into the pool.

There was a flash of light. Ahlia, the Ruling Singer, stood beside her erring daughter. Together, they went down into the pool, and the waters closed above them.

My eyes filled with tears. I knew that this time the Beast was truly gone from me. Still, there was joy in having known her, in all her forms. I looked across the pool at Enderon and smiled.

That being came around toward me. In its hand was the

ring, which I had not seen since I dropped senseless in the hall of Singing.

"You are permitted one possession," the Watcher said. "She left it for you, and you alone of Singers may have so much." The ring slipped onto my finger, and I was warmed with energy and hope.

"Go now, Singer, into the eastward lands. The world of Men is filled with those who have work for you." The dry voice whispered away, and I went across the polished floor, seeing my foreshortened self keeping pace, out through the tunnel, into the night that lay across Orhan.

There were many stars, and I sought out the Eastern Crescent, half-hidden behind the branches of a great Orhan. By it I set my course.

Behind me the faintest of glimmers from the tunnel tickled the snow. Ahead lay an arm of the Wayroad, the mountains, Lirion . . . and all the rest of the world, and the woes of all my kind.